Winter in the Mitten

A collection of writings

by Shiawassee Area Writers

Summit Street Publishing

WINTER IN THE MITTEN
Published by Summit Street Publishing
131 West Grand River
Owosso, Michigan 48867

ISBN 978-0-9905580-8-8

Copyright © 2018

All rights reserved. No part of this book may be reproduced or transmitted in any form or by any means, electronic or mechanical, including photocopying or recording, or by any information storage and retrieval system, without permission in writing from the publisher.

Published in the United States by Summit Street Publishing, Owosso, Michigan.

Cover Art: Jim Edward Hill
Cover Design: Kristy Sweers
Cover Photo: Emily E. Lawson Photography

Printed in the United States of America
2018

10 9 8 7 6 5 4 3 2 1

The Shiawassee Area Writers started in May 2017 to help individuals have a gathering where interaction, collaboration, finding empathy as well as joy, could be found in the process of
writing and publishing.

Starting with eight attendees, the group soon jumped to twenty and now has thirty writers as official members. Meetings include marketing news, group information, a teaching moment, and a hands-on writing exercise. Seasoned writers seek to help those just launching in the process of writing with critiques, helpful hints, and encouragement.

To join us in a meeting, please visit www.shiareawriters.com for meeting dates and times.

Meet the Writers

Pg 1 ~ Prose editor and writer **Jennifer Porter** heralds from Perry. Jennifer is the Prose Editor for The Tishman Review, which helps her bring experience and knowledge to the SAW. Her insight into what is expected from writers in search of publication is much appreciated by our group.

Pg. 10 ~ **Leland Scott's** poems resemble the church hymns of Martin Luther. They bring insight into a deeper world of spiritual meaning, giving glimpses of an ultimate Creator. His winter themed writings entice the reader to find a warm blanket.

Pg. 23 ~ Writer **Barbara Nickels'** family farm experience in this anthology delves into fear, frustration, and panic as a tragic accident sends her family into a winter storm to save the life of her son. She shares fearful life moments through her writings as a farm wife.

Pg. 32 ~ Author **John Morovitz** brings many years of experience to SAW as a writer, as an actor, and director of some great plays staged at the Lebowsky Center. He is also the author of a biography of Owosso native George Hoddy. His wit and insightfulness makes for fun, entertaining memoirs.

Pg. 42 ~ Writer **Brenda Stroub** loves to share her faith in much of her writings and does so with passion and inspiration. Her encouraging words and positive expressions brings hope to her readers.

Pg. 48 ~ Author **Sally Labadie's** passion for picture books comes from her many years of being a professional in education. She has authored nine books and when not writing she loves to search and collect fossils.

Pg. 56 ~ Author **Patti Rae Fletcher** gained her knowledge of children's books through working as a librarian for fifteen years. She is a three-time graduate of the Institute of Children's Literature and has authored a memoir. Presently, Fletcher is the Vice-President of SAW.

Pg. 70 ~ Writer **Linda Perry** not only encourages but supports writers with her time and editing talent. Her memoir piece for this anthology relates her thoughts of starting her first major writing project and how the Christmas of 2017 became her inspiration.

Pg. 79 ~ Author **Laurie Salisbury** enriches the group with her insights and experience in creating children's books. Her stories are wholesome, bringing Godly values to the next generation.

Pg. 83 ~ Poet **Victor Eden** seeks to instill humor into his poetry and the real thoughts of a parent at Christmas. While children expect and await the best, Victor seeks to bring a bit of reality to the season.

Pg. 94 ~ Author **Jason Bullard's** genre places a new slant with his entry. A mysterious, crime-like scene portrays a dysfunctional family celebrating the season at the request of an ailing father.

Pg. 102 ~ Futuristic author **Doug Cornell's** love of writing isn't his only aspiration. Doug enjoys touring the state and the county on a bicycle, often riding his bike to our semi-monthly meetings. Doug is from Corunna.

Pg. 109 ~ Author **Maureen Gilna's** poem is derived from her need to tell children why there are multiple Santa's at Christmas time. Her answer to the problem is found in this anthology.

Pg. 113 ~ So many personalities make up SAW including writer **Tracey Bannister**. Her military experiences bring a whole different perspective to her writing. She shares with us, in this anthology, a submission that catches a glimpse of what it's like to be a soldier ready for her next adventure while keeping her childhood memories intact.

Pg. 117~ Life experiences often fuel our desire to get words on paper. Writer **Jodi Gerona** is one of those writers. Losing a parent is never easy, but Jodi takes her story and shows how God can work through the worst of life to reflect His character.

Pg. 123 ~ Writer **Shawn Gallagher** isn't only learning the craft for herself but endeavors to share her writing expertise with students at her job. Gallagher brings grammar excellence and attention to detail to SAW.

Pg. 132 ~ Writer **Cyndy Habermehl** is a positive and encouraging member of SAW. Her inspiration for writing derives from living on a farm and her childhood memories. The message of love and solid upbringing resonate in her stories. She is from Durand.

Pg. 138 ~ Author **Elizabeth Wehman** is the President/Founder of the Shiawassee Area Writers. Tired of being reclusive in this profession, she made it her mission to find others with the same interest to not only glean from, but to share in the trials and triumphs of being in this chaotic business of putting words onto paper for publication.

Jennifer Porter lives in Perry, Michigan in a historic home with her family, three cats, three dogs, and possibly a pleasant ghost. Her dystopian novella can be found in *The Binge-Watching Cure Anthology*. Her short stories have appeared in *Apeiron Review, Jet Fuel Review, The Dos Passos Review, Hobo Pancakes, Sling Magazine, Ray's Road Review, Gravel Magazine, Old Northwest Review, The Writing Disorder, Fifth Wednesday Journal, Inside the Bell Jar, Journal of Compressed Creative Arts, Meet Cute: A Collection of First Encounters Anthology,* and *Chagrin River Review*. Her essays and memoirs have appeared in *Revolution John, This Zine Will Change Your Life, drafthorse,* and *The Ocotillo Review*. She is a graduate of the University of Michigan and earned her MFA in Writing and Literature from Bennington College in Vermont, where she was a recipient of a Liam Rector Scholarship. She is the co-founding prose editor of *The Tishman Review*, now heading into its fifth year. You can find her at https://butterflymilkweed.wordpress.com. She freelance edits, for more information: jenniferdporter5@gmail.com.

The Paper Route

After we moved back to the metro-Detroit area from São Paulo, Brazil in 1977, my parents mistakenly presumed that if my eleven-year-old brother had a paper route he would learn how to be responsible and work hard. In the most egregious incident while we were overseas, Ricky and his buddy threw rocks onto the curved ceramic tile roofs of some neighborhood houses and the military police became involved. At this time, Brazil was under a military dictatorship and Americans were not their favorite people. My frightened, tearful mother had no idea what to do with Ricky. For many months, there was talk of sending him to an American military boarding school.

My parents grabbed onto the false hope that a paper route would be an important part of the answer for my brother. After all, our papa had a paper route for the very same newspaper, in the very same city, back during the Depression. And look how Papa turned out: a World War II army veteran and successful civil engineer who had built his own house, hammer in hand, on the weekends.

To make matters worse, my parents went on a tour of Europe while Ricky's paper route was to begin. Nana and Papa came to stay with us. Papa oversaw the paper-route teaching deal. Since I was "just a girl," and considered too old at thirteen to be a paper carrier, Nana and I watched Ricky and Papa through the window.

Poor Ricky! It was so early in the morning, and the rain fell cold and steady. But he managed to ride his bicycle to pick up his papers at the drop-off point, and Papa taught him in the garage how to fold them. Ricky had his carrier bag filled with tubes of newspapers. Nana, Papa, and I watched apprehensively as the rain poured down, slicking off Ricky's yellow hooded raincoat.

My brother sat there, one foot on the sidewalk and one foot with his toes on a pedal. Papa grumbled that the papers had to be delivered by a certain time, rain or snow, weekday or weekend. Papa had never missed a single on-time delivery, or so he claimed.

"What is he doing out there?" Papa asked. He had the same tone he used when he caught us kids sneaking up to the television to change the channel while he snored in his recliner. Papa liked to sleep during golf and Tiger baseball games.

Ricky's face contorted into its weird mixture of desperation and anger which made him look like a constipated baby, and we knew he was crying. Not unusual for him but distressing all the same to me and my grandparents. Papa went outside with an umbrella and delivered a pep talk. The weather *was* awful, and I knew Ricky feared this big unknown thing he was supposed to do. But still, it's not like he was facing down the creature of the Black Lagoon. Papa stomped into the garage then into the kitchen.

"Oh dear, Jim," said Nana, her beehive of red hair shifting with concern.

Papa pushed his black plastic glasses against his nose and swept his hand through his salt-n-pepper hair. "I have no idea what is the matter with that kid."

I'm not sure Papa ever realized what his daughter, my mother, put his grandchildren through with her episodes of mental instability and verbal, emotional, and sometimes, physical abuse, but I did.

And lucky for me, I was more like my father. Papa seemed worried about the customers getting their papers on time and I was worried about my brother, so I got on my raincoat and went into the garage. I hopped onto my bicycle and rode to the sidewalk. "Come on," I said to Ricky. "Let's get these papers delivered."

He wiped the snot off his face and set his mouth into a frown. I probably had to talk to him for another five minutes to convince him that with my help, he could deliver the papers. I took over the booklet with the delivery addresses, and he threw the papers on the porch. If there were special instructions, he slipped the paper into a mail slot or left it in a special box. Soaked to the bone, we rushed inside the house to change for school. I think Papa drove us that day. My walk to the middle school was just under one mile.

Over the course of the next several weeks, Ricky got up less and less to do the paper route with me—no matter how loudly I yelled at him while he hid beneath his bed covers. On collection day, he was nowhere to be found.

The newspaper billed its carriers a certain amount of money. The carriers collected a larger amount from the customer and kept the difference. It was good money in my eyes. I kept saying to Ricky, "Are you sure you don't want to make any money?" He was sure. But with the money I could buy books, records, posters, a stereo record player, comic books, and add to my stuffed animal collection. Not just any stuffed animals, the new phenomena of the realistically-designed collector ones, such as a quail (which I still have).

And delivering papers wasn't so bad. There was the mean huge-sounding dog that rammed against the door and ripped the newspaper out of my hand when I stuck it in the slot. I only gave that dog the very end of the paper before I let go. There were creepy customers and obnoxious ones who insisted that I come inside their house. "No thanks," I said, wanting to add, "they haven't caught the Oakland County Child Killer." On occasion, customers refused to pay by never answering their door or responding to notices. The newspaper was good about this, so I still made money for having delivered the paper. And I was very lonely that year. I had been almost entirely rejected (often bullied) at middle school, save for a couple of special kids (one of whom is still my friend). I was overweight, wore glasses, and I could still speak Portuguese. The money bought me things to occupy all that alone time in my bedroom.

I always loved the stillness that followed a heavy snowfall. The world decorated in a sheen of sparkle. If I was lucky, school had been canceled and I had more time to deliver the papers. On just such days, I left my bike in the garage and filled my over-the-shoulder carrier bag with as many papers as possible. I divided my route into sections, returning home to get more papers before heading out again. I trudged through the snowy sidewalks in my clunky winter boots, coat, snow pants, hat, and gloves. My glasses fogged over when my breath escaped the scarf wrapped around my face. The intense hurried walking kept me warm, and I had the mental space to captivate myself with my own imagination. The city slowed and opened unto itself at these times, like a winter wonderland.

It was the last Saturday collection day before Christmas. Snow was piled along the curbs, the sidewalks, the sides of everyone's porch. I had already delivered the paper in the morning, eaten my lunch, and was now back out with my flip-page collection book and pencil.

I dreaded going to Mrs. K's dungeon-like apartment on Fourth Street. For months, she had been inviting me inside to have a cookie. And now she had Christmas cookies. Every time I refused to go in her apartment and eat a cookie, her crestfallen face stung my heart.

Mrs. K was a little old woman who lived in a barely-maintained three-story building built in the 1920s. Her lower-level apartment was in the middle of a moldy hallway with amber-glowing wall lights. The stairwell down was the perfect setting for a B-grade horror movie: dark, steep, no way out.

When Mrs. K answered the door, she stood wavering on her sturdy, no-nonsense shoes, gripping the door knob to keep afloat. I always worried she would keel right over. She wore small round glasses and a ratty house dress with the same sweater, summer and winter. She kept her nylon stockings rolled at her ankles when it was particularly hot.

I could never quite see inside her gloomy apartment from the doorway, and it smelled as if something lay rotten beneath the sofa. Maybe all those uneaten cookies. Or, maybe some dead mice caught in a trap. Or, the body parts of one of the previous newspaper carriers!

I knew Mrs. K needed something from me. Just a few minutes of companionship. Some pleasant interaction with a young person. In all the times, every single week that I collected from her, she never had visitors. But her abject loneliness unsettled me. Is this what happens when we get old? Could this happen to me, when I am already so lonely?

I felt terribly guilty about the tips she gave. I tried to reject the extra money. She insisted. But no matter how bad I felt for her, I could not go inside and have a cookie. Her apartment seemed a tar pit, where my heart would smother in sadness. I didn't think I would survive the encounter.

"How much do I owe you?" she asked. Even though the amount never changed.

She handed me way too much money, more than she'd ever done before. I stared at it for a long time. "Would you like to pay ahead?" Then I wouldn't have to come back and collect for weeks.

She shook her head. "No, it's Christmas. It's your Christmas tip."

"This is too much, Mrs. K. I can't accept it." I pulled out what she owed and tried to hand the rest of the dollar bills back.

She didn't even move. "Would you like to come in for a cookie? I have Christmas cookies. Candy too." She smiled.

I did not want to go in her apartment and find out something that would upset me. Like maybe she didn't have any furniture or enough food to eat or she *really* had no family. Then she would carve out a soft spot on my heart and I would have to visit with her every time I collected. I already had two grandmothers. I didn't need another one.

I stood there with my arm stretched forward, holding those dollar bills in my gloved hand. It was wearing me out. Then Mrs. K said, "You know my son was a paper route boy and now he owns the newspaper. He saved all his tips and look where it got him."

"Your son owns the Grand Maple Tribune?" The paper I delivered?

She nodded with great pride. "I have Christmas cookies. Would you like one?"

I was outraged. He made his own mother pay for *his* newspaper? He lived in the same city and she was always alone? He was rich, and she lived like she did? I could not believe it.

This was not my first rodeo with the inequities of this world. Living in Brazil had shown me abject poverty and despair. My childhood had its own set of lessons, damaging and crippling to both me and my brother. I knew that neither one of my grandmothers would ever be forced to live in a situation like Mrs. K's. My face flushed and I became restless, staring at Mrs. K, trying to figure out what to do. If you don't stand for something, you stand for nothing at all. Injustice always viscerally arose from within my gut, screaming at my brain to do something.

I went into Mrs. K's apartment for a Christmas cookie.

Her entire living space could have fit inside my mother's living room. There was a small sitting area with a decrepit green sofa and a black and white television propped upon a rickety metal stand and a dinky kitchen with a round table for two. Her bedroom was off to the right. A few lamps and light fixtures provided the only light. There was not enough heat for the bitter winter day. Her furnishings were as threadbare as her clothes.

She showed me the candy dish on an end table, filled with one single glob of old-fashioned hard Christmas candies, like my grandma loved. I could not get one candy separated enough from the glob to get it out of the dish.

"How about a cookie instead?" she asked. She had hobbled into the kitchen and sat down.

I took off my hat and walked over. I hesitated, my hand over the plate, trying to discern how many decades the cookies had been in her apartment.

"I just bought them," she said. "In case you finally came in."

I took a bite of a tree-shaped sugar cookie with green sprinkles.

Then she proceeded to tell me all about her "wonderful" son, walking me around the apartment while I nibbled at my cookie, showing me newspaper clippings and photos of him that she'd framed.

We wished each other Merry Christmas when I finally left.

To be fair to the son, as the months passed by and I visited Mrs. K every collection day, I realized that he did care, at least a little bit. One Saturday, I just missed him, Mrs. K said. And other Saturdays she had me help her put groceries away that he'd dropped off.

And being the age I am now, I understand that there might be a side of the story that only he could tell. A side that might explain how it is that we can love someone but need to protect ourselves from them. That sometimes, we have to let people be how they choose to be and do for them the best we can, and that one of the hardest things to do in life, is to be merciful to those who have hurt us the most.

Leland Scott was raised in rural Michigan. He began a military career in the Navy in 1956, serving as an instructor and pursuing a career in drafting. After twenty years of service, he retired and returned to civilian life in Michigan, with his wife and four children.

As a civilian, he used his vocational training to follow a trade of drafting and teaching. Working in engineering firms, Leland taught in business meetings and part-time in community college. He then taught at Baker College of Owosso for 22 years. He now maintains a part-time business designing homes.

Leland began writing while in the Navy, writing poetry about his experiences. He entered a navy-wide essay contest with one of his poems, *What is an American,* and was the winner of the Freedom Foundation award and George Washington Medal. In 2006, published a poetry book, *Special Moments in Poetry* using the pen-name of Lescott.

Leland also published a textbook, *BASIC DRAFTING a manual for beginning drafters,* which is being sold internationally. While faculty at Baker College, Leland was awarded the Instructor of the Year award. He was also named the College Poet Laureate and wrote for a monthly poetry column in the college paper.

Leland continues to write poetry, music, and short stories.

Leland received an MBA at Baker College, a Bachelor's degree from John Wesley College, a Vocational Education Teaching Certificate from the University of Maryland, Teaching Certificate from the U. S. Navy, and diplomas from two Navy Drafting schools. Leland also attended William and Mary College, Old Dominion College, and Lansing Community College.

In Search of a Home

Lance pulled into the first gas station he saw as he entered the little town of Richland. A light snow was falling. His nearly bald tires were going to be a problem if that kept up. He had been driving most of the day. His old truck needed gas and there was steam coming from under the hood. As he lifted the hood, he could see where the steam was coming from – a tiny hole in a radiator hose spewed like a mini-geyser.

"That don't look good," came a voice from over his shoulder. He turned to see a young woman in a dirty ball cap and a grease-covered shirt, wiping her hands with a rag not much cleaner than her coveralls.

"Yeah, I guess I better get a new hose pretty quick."

"I can put one on for you," she offered.

"That would be great!"

"You can gas up and then pull it over there." She pointed to a spot in front of a large garage door. Lance followed her instructions then went inside. She was leafing through a large catalog on the counter.

"My name is Lance – Lance Cooper," he offered. She barely looked up from her search. "Glad to meet you, I'm Joan. It'll take a little while; I don't have the right hose, but I can call and get it brought over."

"Okay. How long will it take, and how much?"

"Twelve seventy-five installed, and I expect about a half hour to get it here. It has to come from the auto parts store over in Dexter."

"Okay, I guess." Lance said uncertainly. He noticed that it was getting late in the day and he was tired. "Any place to get a room in town?"

"No motels, but Mrs. Jameson rents out rooms sometimes. I'll call her if you like."

"Sure. It would just be for one night." Joan made a quick phone call and nodded. "Yep, she would be glad to have you."

"Thanks. Just point the way."

Joan excused herself to take care of a gas customer, then came back to Lance. "Where are you heading, Lance?"

"I don't really know," he replied. Joan looked at him quizzically.

"I mean, I'm just looking for a place to settle. I just got out of the service, got no real home to go to and thought I'd just drive across country lookin' for some place. I bought this old pickup from a sailor who was going to sea and here I am a civilian with no place to go!"

"You were in the service? What branch?"

"Navy. I just got discharged in Norfolk."

"Really? My dad was in the Navy! We lived in Norfolk when I was little. I don't remember it much. He was like you, had no place to go when he got out. We came here and he bought this place and we've been here ever since. We pump gas and do some mechanic work. I help out a lot. He has been laid up, so I am pretty much running the place right now."

"Sorry to hear about your dad. I guess he is lucky to have you."

"Yeah, I'm the only son he never had," she said with a wink. "I can do small jobs, like oil changes and stuff like yours. He does the big stuff when he's able."

"Can you recommend a good place to eat?"

"There are a couple of bars in town that serve good food. We just got a fast-food place on the other end of town, Casey's, that has pretty good burgers. They're all right here on Main street. If you drive on the way you were going, you'll find 'em."

Lance settled into a chair and browsed the magazines on the table beside him while he waited for the hose to be installed. By the time Lance should have had his repairs and been on his way, the snowfall had increased and his radiator hose had not arrived. Joan noticed that he was getting restless and offered a solution.

"Lance, sorry about the delay. I've got an idea. I can tape that hose up like a band-aid and you can drive with it tonight and come back tomorrow. Okay?"

Lance agreed and settled back in his chair to wait. Joan hurried out toward the truck, tape in hand. When she returned, Lance asked directions and headed off to Mrs. Jameson's. He found the house without any trouble.

"Just like she said," he muttered to himself, "Big brick house, just around the corner to the right on Watkins street."

He parked in front and approached the front door, duffle bag in hand. Mrs. Jameson met him at the door and immediately led him to a room just off the entrance. It had a dresser, a big bed, a rocking chair and a door that led to a small bathroom. Lance said it would be fine and started to go in. Mrs. Jameson quickly turned and led him, instead, down the hall. Lance followed. He liked her right away. She was a small plump lady in her sixties, grey-brown hair pulled up into a bun at the back of her head, and an infectious smile that often bubbled into a cheerful little laugh that made him feel comfortable.

"You can have a key, if you want," she said, "but you won't need it. We don't lock doors much around here." She continued to talk as they walked. "I don't make meals for my guests, but I want to show you the kitchen. There's a coffee pot and cookies in the cookie jar."

Lance turned to leave, but she offered him a cup of coffee and pointed to the cookie jar. She sat down at a big wooden table. He took the coffee and a cookie and sat across from her. Mrs. Jameson chattered on, asking Lance about his trip and where he was headed. He told her the same as he had Joan, and she started off in a new direction.

"You came just in time for the Christmas festival!" she started. Apparently Joan hadn't told her that he only planned to be here one night, but he listened politely as she went on. "I know Christmas is more than two weeks away, but we open the season with a celebration – this weekend with a parade and tree lighting . . ." she went on, extolling the wonders of Christmas in Richland. Lance found a pause and rose to go. He thanked her for the coffee, and said he was going to go find some supper. It didn't seem to dampen the description of the coming event. "You will really enjoy it," she said with a big smile as she followed him to the door, and watched after him as he left.

***

On his way to his truck, Lance met Joan on the sidewalk. She didn't look the same all cleaned up, wearing jeans and a puffy down-filled vest, with a bright red scarf wrapped around her neck. That greasy ball cap was gone to expose wavy ash-blonde hair down almost to her shoulders. He almost didn't recognize her.

"I wanted to let you know that the hose came in. It came just after you left. You can come in the morning and I'll install it. Did you find Casey's?"

"Not yet. I was just heading out to find it."

"Want some company?"

"Sure, your car or mine?"

"I'll drive. I know the way, and I've got the jeep. It will do better in the snow than your bald tires," she joked. On the way, Joan pointed out the various shops – the bakery, the hardware, drugstore, and grocery. "Most everything is right here on Main street, except for the mill and the school and, of course, the river."

"River?"

"Yeah, the river is our big attraction. It's down that road that we just passed. That's one reason Dad stayed here. He likes to boat and fish. Actually, there is a river and a lake. The river widens into a big man-made lake just below town. We have quite a marina down there. Since you're a sailor, you might like it. I hear they are looking for help."

***

Casey's was busy. Joan suggested they just go through the drive-through and eat in the jeep. "We can drive down to the river and eat there."

They got their order and she drove back to the river road, pointing out town features as she drove. "The school is the other way, up the hill," she said as she turned toward the river.

At the marina, she turned to drive along parallel to the river and parked in a spot facing the water, where they talked as they ate. Lance had a good view of the marina along the river and toward the lake; just as Joan had described it.

"For a small town, you have a lot of boats."

"Well, we have a lot of out-of-towners who use the marina. Some come from quite a distance."

"Does your dad have a boat here?"

"Sure, two of them – one for fishing and a pontoon for the family."

"So, I meant to ask about your father. You said he was laid up. Is it serious?"

"Not really," she shrugged. "He strained his back and the doctor made him take some time off and rest. He'll be back at it again soon, I am sure. Oh, hey! Did Mrs. Jameson tell you about the Christmas Festival?"

"Yeah, in great detail."

"I can't imagine that she wouldn't. She is a big supporter of the event. Did she talk you into staying for it?"

"Naw, I'm not into such things much."

"Oh, why not? Don't you believe in Christmas?"

"Oh, no, it's not that. It just seems like it's a family thing, y'know?"

"I understand. You got no family to go home to?"

"Not really. I never knew my dad, and Mom died while I was in the navy. I have a sister out in California, but she's a lot older. We were never very close."

"Well, you might consider staying here a while," Joan said, as she turned the jeep around and headed back. At Mrs. Jameson's, she reminded him that he could come get his truck fixed anytime in the morning, and waved a smiling good-bye.

***

It was early morning when Lance said good-bye to Mrs. Jameson over a cup of coffee. She urged him to stay for the Christmas Festival, but to no avail. He put his bag in the truck and headed back to the gas station. It didn't take long to get the hose on, and he was ready to continue on his journey. He thanked Joan for her help as she also repeated the suggestion that he stay for the Christmas Festival. She wished him well on his trip and his search as he climbed into his truck and drove off.

Lance thought about the events of the day before. He couldn't understand it, but he felt funny leaving. He suddenly had a strange nostalgic feeling but brushed it off as he drove through town past the shops and scenes that Joan had shown him last evening. The town looked all Christmassy and quiet, covered in snow. But the sun was shining, the road was clear, and the world lay before him. He passed Casey's and the city limits, driving up a long hill that took him westward. At the top of the hill, there was a 'look-out' with a parking spot. Lance pulled in and surveyed the view below – the river, the lake, and back at the town. He sat for a long time just drinking it in, then turned the truck around and headed back toward Richland.

A Winter Walk

Early in the morning, when the earth was yet quite still
I walked across the meadow, o'er frozen pond and up the hill

The air was cool and misty, brushing soft against my face
and from the darkened heavens floated down a fluffy flake.

I stopped to view my footprints in the newly fallen snow
and overhead the clouded sky that somehow seemed to glow

The dawn was yet quite hidden behind that hovering sky
and eerie shadows spoke of things not yet clear to eye.

I saw a field mouse scurry between some barren stalks
as tho' in a desperate hurry to be home from a searching walk

I wished to linger longer – the moment to prolong
I wished to somehow capture the peaceful silent song.

But as the skies grew lighter and the shadows slowly dimmed
The world around me wakened as tho' life returned again

Retracing snow-filled footprints, I wound my way back home
to join again reality with my memories – mine alone.

The Creator's Touch

I think when it's winter
the creator looks down
and sees His drab earth
with a bit of a frown.

He takes out His paintbrush
and touches the scene
He paints the world white
where it used to be green.

He takes tiny snowflakes
and piles them up
atop of each fence post
like foam on a cup.

He decorates branches
and evergreen trees
and smoothes it all out
with a wintry breeze.

The Christmas Story

Tis' the myst'ry of all time
quite like a fairy tale;
yet wrapped in hist'rys pages
with a truth that does prevail.

A simple virgin maiden
gave birth to a little boy
in a stable quite unnoticed
tho' angels sang of joy.

Local shepherds came to visit
and bowed before the child.
while looking on so proudly
his father surely smiled.

A gift sent down from heaven
- the son of God above
to be a sacrifice for sin
an example of God's love.

This birth had been long promised
by prophets of the land
tho' they didn't recognize him
- they expected a monarch grand.

This baby's name was Jesus
and he lived to preach and heal
was crucified, yet lived again
by breaking death's strong seal.

Tho' some reject the story
it's remembered 'round the earth
by yearly celebrations
of that single baby's birth.

There's something almost magic
that the Christmas season brings
decorations, shopping, giving
and the music that we sing.

The stars seem somehow brighter
to remind us of that day
when a star shone over Bethlehem
guiding wise men on their way.

It's really not a mystery
to all who do believe
and celebrate the birth of Christ
on that far off Christmas Eve.

Barbara Nickels has been writing for over fifty years, both fiction and non-fiction. Her interests include, published short stories and newspaper articles as well as submissions to various publications and magazines. She and her husband graduated from Michigan State University's College of Agriculture and Natural Resources in 1991. She mainly focused on English Literature subjects. For over ten years they wintered in sunny Florida where Barbara enjoyed her years as Editor/Publisher of the Retirement Village Newsletter. She and her husband live near Corunna in Central Michigan. You can contact this author at bobbienickels@gmail.com.

The Bullfighter

The dawning of January, 1978 ushered in not only the worst snowstorm in the county's history but also brought with it something that shook our family to the core and changed our lives forever.

Early that snowy January morning Irv went out the back door only to sink to his knees in drifts covering the open doorway. "Jeepers, Creepers!" he shouted. After freeing his dad from the pile of snow, our son Curt proceeded to shovel a path from the back door toward the cow barn. "This is the heaviest, wettest snow I can remember," he muttered as he huffed and puffed, swinging the shovel, snow flying into heavy drifts on each side.

Irv continued getting the milking, feeding and watering done as usual for the day. The number one priority of course was to begin with breakfast. While eating, our talk was interrupted by a voice coming over the radio: *'This is the Shiawassee County road commissioner. We have an urgent message for every citizen of Shiawassee County. It is imperative that you follow these instructions completely in order to insure your family's safety.*

The sheriff's office has issued a warning to stay off all primary as well as secondary roads in Shiawassee County until further notice. Please stay tuned to this station for further updates. Thank you for your cooperation.'

Of course this dampened the spirits of everyone. We discussed the situation as it affected the farm as well as our neighbors.

After breakfast each one headed outside to their assigned tasks. Eight-year-old Matthew eagerly put on his snowsuit and outdoor gear after his dad told him he could ride with him as they plowed the driveways. Together they left the house and went to the pole barn. With

Matt secure in the jump seat beside Irv on the tractor they began plowing.

Later Irv told me Matt got bored and asked if he could play in the drifts making a snow fort. His dad told him to hop down and stay safe within sight then continued plowing while keeping a watchful eye on the boy happy at work building his project.

Turning the tractor around in order to clear a different area, Irv glanced toward the spot where Matt had been playing just a few minutes before. Not seeing any activity he stopped, got off the tractor and walked to the pole barn. He looked in the barn and glimpsed Matt against the wall of the manger. Running over he saw Matt lying against the manger boards, eyes closed. "Son, can you hear me?" he asked. Matt opened his eyes and moaned, "I was just digging my fort. Boots walked up behind me and butted me, knocking me against the manger. I can't breathe!"

Our yearling bull Boots was a gentle giant. He loved getting his head rubbed by anyone who wandered near the barnyard fence. Thus far he had been a welcome addition to the farm family.

But what happened today? And why did this happen, Irv asked himself. He scooped Matt up in his arms and hurried to the house, bursting into the kitchen as he called out to me.

I held Matt in my arms while his dad stomped loudly to the wall phone and proceeded to try to get a hold of someone who could come to the farm to help us or at least direct us to the hospital. He was put through to the county road commissioner immediately.

I only heard one side of the conversation but could hear the urgency in Irv's voice as he explained the situation. Earlier he tried to drive the truck out the driveway. Impossible! He got stuck the first few attempts.

Irv hung up the phone and turned slowly to face me. "He said there is nothing anyone can do at this time to help. The county is under a lockdown. Nothing is moving out there. However the commissioner said if we can get three miles east to Newburg road, they can plow an ambulance through from Owosso to that point and meet us. That is the best they can offer for help."

Irv walked to the door then turned to me and said "Get yourself bundled up, Barb. And please get a couple of blankets to wrap around Matt for the trip. No telling what we'll run into on the way."

He went to the garage and started warming the truck for the journey. He returned to the house, scooped Matt up and we headed outside. In the truck Irv embraced both of us. We bowed our heads and quietly prayed. Out the driveway we went, not knowing how far we'd get or whether we would make it all the way to the hospital. The truck bucked and jerked through impossible drifts as we fought the snow. At the corner Irv looked down the road, not seeing either the county plow or flashing lights of an ambulance. He glanced at me and said, "I'm making the decision to go by way of the shortest route, which is State road. This is our best chance to reach the hospital. Ready? Here we go!"

Praying all the way down State road, we couldn't believe we got through to Corunna. It seemed to take forever while driving. Irv found strength to keep the steering straight and the wheels from sliding into the ditch. We bucked drifts over the top of the truck's hood. Seeing a huge drift ahead Irv stopped, shifted again and gunned the engine. Full speed ahead.

As we drove, both of us noticed the snow spraying over the top of the truck's hood. It looked like angels holding their wings outstretched, moving the mountain of white. So beautiful. I'll never forget the sight. All the while Matt lay still, his head in Irv's lap and torso and legs draped across my lap. His face was white as snow.

"There is the Corunna city limit sign" Irv said. "We made it so far." The eeriness of the last leg of this harrowing journey was unreal. Streets were deserted, every last one. Not a vehicle in sight. But we knew we were not alone.

We continued to M-21 in complete isolation and silence. We were completely alone on the road at noon on a Friday.

Irv seemed to feel better by marking our progress to the hospital out loud. Soon we were turning onto the street to the hospital.

Suddenly we were sliding sideways up to the front entrance of the hospital. Doctors came running out with a gurney, ready to load up the patient.

A new doctor with only one year's practice under his belt, Dr. Call had been the second phone call Irv placed that morning. He told Irv at that time that he would walk the half mile from his home north of the hospital and meet us since his driveway as well as every street between was blocked.

At the door the hospital personnel told us, "So far today we have been sending our shift nurses and doctor's home by way of the National Guard in ATV's and trucks. How in the world did you get here on these blocked roads?"

We didn't have time to answer them. Nor could we have explained all of it anyway. They whisked the gurney through the double glass doors. A mountain of paperwork to fill out awaited us as soon as we arrived and we could see a flurry of activity as people dressed in scrubs worked surrounding Matt. Dr. Call and several other doctors were working to stabilize him. Matthew lay very still on the table.

A nurse came by and explained to us that our boy was in shock and they were working to find a vein that hadn't collapsed.

The room was aptly named; we waited – and waited – and waited for what seemed the longest time. We watched through the glass as they wheeled in a portable x-ray machine. I don't know if that was such a good idea for us to watch every move in the adjoining room. The verdict is still out forty years later.

Irv sat quietly, watching the scene unfold through the glass before us. I kept busy going into the bathroom to vomit, wash my face and pray, in that order.

About an hour later, Dr. Call joined us. "I won't mince words with you guys," he said gently. "Everyone has been working diligently to keep Matt from crashing in there. He's in shock and they are still trying to find a good vein in order to start the I.V. Once the fluid drip is in place, we begin working on that collapsed lung."

"It is pretty serious right now, but we are all pulling for your family to get some good news pretty quick." He continued, "The x-ray shows he has not only a collapsed lung but also bleeding is coming from his belly into the lungs. And the spleen has a large tear. We think that's the culprit. We need to get him stabilized in order to give him the best chance in surgery later."

He paused and studied our faces. I wanted to scream and I am sure Irv felt the same by the way he squeezed my hand. Irv told Dr. Call we trusted his judgment in this.

They moved Matt to intensive care soon after that. Later a nurse came to the waiting room and told us we could go upstairs and sit with Matt until they could prepare for surgery. We sat beside his bed, listening to the beeps and whistles coming from machines at the head of his bed.

Assorted wires stuck out from his body; he was hog-tied and helpless. We felt the same way.

We both must have dozed off. Sometime in the middle of the night we awakened as the doctor came into the room and walked over to Matt's bedside. "I don't know what to tell you,' he began. "We just completed another x-ray. It shows Matt's spleen has stopped bleeding and seems stable. I cannot explain this, or why he is stable now. He's sleeping peacefully. Dr. Ford has been standing by in order to do the surgery. However, all of us agree that surgery is not indicated at this time."

"We're not out of the woods by any means. His lung is still collapsed, but we can deal with that later. Matt will be in intensive care for at least a week."

"If it's all right with you, I want to call in Dr. McKnight tomorrow. He is retired but I want his opinion as to ongoing treatment. I also want him to examine Matt regarding a plan to get that lung inflated." We agreed with him. He knew when to ask for help. This gave us hope.

The next morning Matt's room became medical information central. Almost every doctor and nurse at Memorial stopped by to see him.

One morning Dr. Ford came by to see how Matt was doing. He said, "So how is the little bullfighter doing today?" From that day on Matt became known as 'The Bullfighter.'

But that stubborn lung still remained deflated.

Dr. McKnight came by that night to check Matt and told us a very unusual story. In WWII doctors at medical units discovered through trial and error an unusual method of re-inflating wounded soldiers' collapsed lungs. Surgeons took large glass bottles and inserted rubber tubes in the top of the sterile bottles, the other end placed through incision into the injured lung.

He said, "I would like to try this on him since nothing else has worked up to this point. What do you both think?" Irv replied, "Let's give it a try. What do we have to lose?"

Down to the old basement of the hospital the doctor went, rummaged around for quite a while and finally came up with a large glass bottle (it looked like the type of bottle used for bottled water dispensers). He added new rubber tubing to the mix.

Dr. Call related the following to us the next morning:

The night before, Dr. McKnight had the staff sterilize the old equipment carefully. Talking as he proceeded, the doctor explained the procedure:

"OK, first I'm making an 'x' above the lung, now I'm placing the tube over the incision. In goes the tube over the incision. Now I will position it and pray to God it works," he said.

The ancient procedure and equipment did the trick. Success. The lung re-inflated beautifully despite many warnings from hospital personnel to the contrary. Matt remained in intensive care under close supervision for a week. 'Just in case,' the doctors said.

In time he was moved downstairs to a regular room for an additional week.

When Matt's follow-up doctor appointment came, the doctor spent a lot of time with his stethoscope listening to Matt's vitals. Finally he pronounced the good news. "Not only is he as good as before, he is better than new." Welcome words.

Today Matt is the picture of good health. He's fine except for the perfect, white cross etched on his chest.

John E. Morovitz is an eighty-four year old retired physician who refers to himself as a "recreational writer." Much of his literary dabbling has been satirical, sometimes nonsensical poetry and essays for friends' special events. On occasion he has composed poignant eulogies and commemorative verse. As an author with minimal formal training, he "writes as he reads," non-critically; for entertainment or to learn something. He lacks obsessive concerns for the myriad  of arbitrary rules of the authorities. He is literally an editor's nightmare.

John's only significant work is a self-published mini-biography of a much beloved industrialist and philanthropist, Mr. George Hoddy. Pending for some time, has been a family memoir that focuses on the Christian love that overcame the rampant post-war hatred of the Japanese.

These stories, herein included, would not likely have been written were it not for the encouragement and support of new-found friends at Shiawassee Area Writers. As a diversion, writing has competed with avidity for gardening, golfing, and Community Theater.

John Morovitz

The Alpha Female's Jinx

When my younger sister Carolyn was born I was a week from turning four. Ruthie, the eldest of our trio of sibs, was already six. Through the middle school years she was always quite mature and of good size for her age. As a matter of fact, she not only towered over all of my friends, but also most of the boys in her class. It hurts to admit it, but there were a few occasions, often exaggerated by her, when she did use her size advantage to defend her puny "baby brother." I think she actually got some sadistic pleasure in beating up boys. She was what I now would call an "alpha female."

While I wouldn't exactly say Ruthie was my parents' favorite, she did most definitely command their complete confidence. "Dear sweet Ruthie" could do no wrong. I was sure they never realized that in their rare absences, their angel ruled the house like a Russian Tsarina, bossing us around, and demanding angelic discipline. She was ever eager to report any perceived infractions. It seems only natural that Carolyn and I longed for the day when our big sister would receive her due.

****

Christmas was only a couple of weeks away, and our house was beautifully bedecked inside and out. Two days earlier we had made our annual excursion to find the "perfect tree." As usual, Dad had picked the coldest, most blustery night for the family trek. For excited kids any nice tree would do, but for our father the selection process bordered on exact science. "A Morovitz tree" had to be tall enough to reach our eight-foot-ceiling, and have a poker-straight trunk. Full at the base, with no thin areas, it had to taper to a perfect cone. Of course, it had to be of good color and be able to retain its needles. Quite predictably, no such specimen was ever to be found on the first four or five lots. This year was no exception.

Eventually the lofty expectations ebbed and the search ended. The freezing cold and wind-driven snow showers discouraged three weary kids from once more leaving the auto's warmth. Our intrepid patriarch, however, finally thought he had found what he had been seeking. With help, he secured the hulking evergreen to the roof of the car and we headed for the comfort of home.

It was no great surprise to any of us that the top of the nine-and-a half footer had to be trimmed, and a foot and a half removed from the base, just to get the thing in the house. Its grand entrance had to be delayed a day because melting snow kept dripping from it. Once inside, the trunk required considerable shaving to fit into its stand. Unnoticed in the darkness the night before was the trunk's significant scoliosis. Shimming was necessary to restore an image of erectness. So much for the science of shopping, but at least we had our tree, and as usual, when it was fully lit and adorned we were oblivious to any of mother-nature's flaws. Soon too, we were forgetful of our suffering the previous night.

After supper, a day later, mom and Ruthie were doing dishes. The rest of us were in the living room, probably listening to "The Lone

Ranger," and admiring our festive handiwork. We heard rising voices as Ruthie stormed from the kitchen toward the stairway to the bedroom we still shared. In a fit of rage, she was wildly flailing her dish towel, brushing the tree as she passed. The helpless conifer tumbled over onto the floor, shedding its ornaments around the room.

Inside, as evil as it may sound, I was secretly waiting for that moment when the alpha female would finally be getting hers. How shocking and disappointing it was to see that pathetic, hysterically sobbing, apologetic creature being hugged and consoled by both parents. "That's alright sweetheart." "It's only a tree." "We know you didn't mean to do it."

Life just doesn't seem fair sometimes.

I never realized the impact that incident must have had on her at the time, and over the years when she was occasionally reminded of it. I'm not sure if it was some lingering guilt, or the nostalgia of how our dear parents reacted. After all it wasn't a capital crime. Trees get knocked over all the time.

****

It was almost exactly seventy years later when a few family members gathered for a Sunday dinner at the home of our daughter Amy. The house was handsomely attired for the approaching holidays. Its cathedral ceiling easily accommodated the eleven-foot balsam that highlighted the living room.

With us that day were Aunt Ruthie and Uncle Frank. My sister was less than a month from her eightieth birthday. Long ago having shed my boyhood image of the alpha female, she had metamorphosed into a sweet, and gentle, and caring friend. Quite late in life she had resumed piano lessons in the hope of reviving the notable skills of her youth.

After the meal we reconvened in the living room to enjoy our coffee. Once more we sat appreciating the beauty of the towering evergreen framed by a huge picture window and the snow covered landscape outside. With minimal coaxing, Ruthie began fingering the keys of Amy's spinet. The sound of our carols and the flickering flame and crackling from the fireplace completed a Norman Rockwell scene of holiday warmth. There were no rowdy kids or frolicking pets to disturb the pleasant ambience. As if mesmerized, we sat almost motionless enjoying the moment.

Without warning the serenity was broken when the giant balsam, apparently tired of standing, keeled over in the direction of our stunned pianist. The music ceased, and like the ten-year-old girl so long ago, my aging sister's eyes began to glisten as she became distraught and apologetic. "I'm sorry." "It's my fault." "It must have been my playing." "I'm so sorry."

Only after much consolation and reassurance that she was not some kind of Christmas tree jinx did she calm herself down and resume her music. Still in the holiday spirit, the rest of us quietly retrieved the ornaments and righted the mischievous, troublesome tree… "It's alright sweetheart." "It's only a tree." "No one meant it to happen."

Our Christian Snowmen

The predicted snow showers had already begun to coat the roads with a thin layer of white as Joanne, Linda, and I pulled away from our cottage on Silver Lake. The end of March was fast approaching, bringing the perennial hope of an early spring. The nuisance of such late season precipitation, however, is not an unusual phenomenon in the Traverse City area. As a rule it does not interrupt the planned activities of the hearty souls who inhabit northwestern Lower Michigan. We most definitely had plans for the evening.

By the time we reached the home of our daughter Susan, only twelve miles away, there was already about three inches of accumulation. During supper, through the glass slider door, we watched the large white flakes continue their descent. The eager anticipation of the grandkids was evident, especially ten-year-old Makenna. Her two older brothers, Ty and A J, seemed a bit more reserved, as macho boys are supposed to be. We adults hoped not to disappoint them.

After the meal, a reassessment of the situation outside, and some serious deliberation, we decided it was not unreasonable to attend the performance of "Doctor Dolittle." The decision was not made lightly, in spite of an additional couple inches of the white stuff. We had purchased the tickets weeks earlier for this final weekend of the show's run, so it was now or never. The Old Town Playhouse was less than a fifteen minute drive. Maybe it was just wishful thinking that the weather might be letting up some.

When we reached the old converted church house at the corner of Eighth and Cass we were reassured that we were not the only fearless or foolhardy stalwarts willing to brave the now seven plus inches of snow. Even on the areas that had been shoveled earlier, it was difficult for the twelve and fourteen-year-old boys to maneuver their Aunt Linda's wheelchair which has given her mobility since early childhood. Fortunately, a grade level door provided access to a small elevator that would raise her to the main auditorium.

As expected, it was an exciting and imaginative performance that earned the standing ovation from the full house of intrepid patrons who then had to exit into a good foot-deep blanket of white. With some difficulty I moved our vehicle to the front of the theater where I impatiently had to wait. It was embarrassing to be obstructing the egress of others, as I repeatedly cleared the car's windows and lights. After several minutes the family appeared, having been delayed by an elevator malfunction, requiring Linda to "butt-walk" down the stairs and the boys to carry the chair.

Sue and the kids, with their four-wheel drive Jeep, were better prepared for a treacherous return home. We, on the other hand, knew our two-wheel drive Traverse would face a more daunting challenge. Wisely, we took a longer route using more traveled streets, but upon reaching our somewhat rural setting we found no ruts in the fourteen-inch covering on Roman Drive. The latter is the only access to the peninsula that juts into the middle of the lake. The absence of any street-lighting and the wildly swirling flakes in our headlights significantly impaired my vision and orientation. With no other option and trepidation approaching panic, I crept along. Though she said nothing, Joanne's uneasiness convinced me she joined me in questioning the wisdom of our earlier decision. Soon, to our dismay, we would learn…the worst was yet to come.

The initial sense of relief we felt at the sight of our home, less than two-hundred yards ahead was quickly aborted by the sickening sensation of the car sliding sideways off the road, to become totally paralyzed in a large drift. My shoveling and attempts to push were futile.

It was now near one a.m. when my weary, eighty-year-old body began wading through the knee deep white stuff to at last reach our surprisingly dark abode. I was sure we had left the exterior lights on. After fumbling for keys, I entered a room not much warmer than the out-of-doors. A total power outage, what next? I groped my way to the kitchen to find a flashlight. I called Susie to check on them and inquire the location of the small toboggan sled. Retrieving it from the rafters of the cluttered detached garage wasn't easy, but soon, with it in tow and a feeling of renewed confidence, I retraced my deep tracks to rescue Joanne and Linda, still snug and warm inside of the marooned automobile.

We managed to get our paraplegic daughter onto the sled, only to watch it and Linda capsize into the snow covered brush. Our reflexive laugh was quickly quelled by the struggle we had getting Linda back onto her wheel-less chariot. Even more disheartening was the reality that Joanne and I were unable to even budge the sled.

The time was now approaching two o'clock. The futility of even getting Linda back into the car began to induce a feeling of desperation, and a fear of spending a few more hours out in the mini-blizzard. Even a call to 911 wasn't likely to bring prompt assistance.

Suddenly our fretful pondering was eased by a pair of headlights entering the peninsula behind us. Like the "Star of Bethlehem," they were guiding the speeding compact toward us in the tracks we had created the hour before. "Please let them stop," was the silent prayer of three.

The two young men, in their early twenties, who emerged from the car, asked if they could help. I saw no wings or halos but indeed they were a godsend.

After moving their vehicle up the gentle slope of Roman Drive, they returned with something more to put over Linda. As the two boys pulled, and I pushed we were only able to gain about twenty feet between frequent brief pauses to catch our breath. It was well after two when we finally reached the house and got our also weary passenger safely inside. Joanne, only three years my junior, bad knees and all, somehow managed to follow in our path.

Much relieved, with our mission complete, I reached for my wallet to reward our young rescuers for their Good Samaritan deeds.

"Oh no sir, we can't take money, we're Christians."

Taken aback I responded, "We're Christians too, but you saved our lives. Well then, how about a brewsy?" There was no hesitation in their response. So in the wee hours of that morning, in my unheated living room, lighted only by the reflection off of the whitened lake outside, we chatted, as each of us downed a couple cold ones.

As the boys were about to leave, I was able to slip my remaining few twenties into one of their open pockets. They departed into the darkness from whence they had come. Rapidly becoming covered by the unrelenting snow, they soon blended into their surroundings as they slowly blazed a new trail toward home. By the light of a new day we would find more than twenty-one inches to deal with.

Fully clothed, Joanne and Linda huddled together under layers of blankets, while I dozed on the floor in front of the fireplace I tended. With all that happened on that memorable and frightening eve, and the dimness of light that precluded good vision, I regret I did not record the boys' names or where they lived up the street. To my awareness I have not seen them since. Within my aging memory they shall forever remain our heaven-sent "Christian Snowmen."

Brenda Stroub is a born again Christian who wants to share Christ's love with others. She has always enjoyed writing memoirs, journaling, taking notes, and doing outlines. Being a part of the Shiawassee Area Writers group has been a very rewarding, and educational experience for her. A great release of giving back, a portion of what she has been given; a process full of blessings.

Brenda has previously been employed as a secretary, office manager, payment solutions coordinator, and a Certified Dental Practice Management Administrator. Another way she loves to communicate to the world is through sign language. She was a deaf interpreter at church for three years, and has taught sign language as well.

Brenda was born in Flint, and graduated from Durand High School. She has also lived in Dayton, and now resides in Lennon with her husband, Kip. They have two adult children and ten grandchildren.

The Christmas Gift

At twenty-one years old, I began to search for a deeper meaning of life. My husband led me to the greatest Christmas gift of all. I believed in God as the Creator, but my life felt so empty, with no real peace. I had no clue what it meant to be a Christian, but my husband did. He shared with me about people he knew that were real Christians. He said the light of Christ shined through their lives and they lived like their existence depended on a personal relationship with Christ.

Some close friends of ours came over to invite us to church and shared with us how Jesus Christ had changed their lives. I wanted to hear more, so I went to their church. It was the Sunday before Christmas, and I'd just had our first baby in November; an early Christmas gift from God.

Pastor Drury gave a sermon about how God loved us so much that He gave us the precious gift of His Son on Christmas day. He said we just need to accept His gift, repent of our sins, and believe Jesus rose from the dead. Then He would wash us clean, never leave us, and give us eternal life.

I wanted so much to give my life to God as a living sacrifice and make that my Christmas gift back to Him. Stepping out in faith to trust in Jesus at that moment was such a new thought to me, I let my fear hold me back. But three months later, I was ready. In bed that night, I placed my life in God's hands and asked Jesus into my heart. It was a huge step of faith and the beginning of a wonderful journey I could never have imagined. It was a Christmas gift that keeps on giving.

As the years pass, I have seen prayers answered and so much in my life has changed. I am still a work in progress and through it all I've learned nothing is impossible with God. He works all things together for the good. Now I know who I believe in and am confident that I can depend on Him. By trusting in Jesus, I have witnessed miracles only God can do. It has been, and still is, an amazing adventure. I am so thankful for all He has brought me through.

He took me:

-from unclean to clean,

- from sinful to forgiven,

-from lost to found,

-from blind to sight,

-from dead to life,

-from sad to glad,

-from empty to full,

-from drowning to saved,

-from darkness to light,

-from chaos to peace,

Glory, glory, what a story!

You make my heart sing!

Praises, praises to my King!

If you haven't already done so, please take a moment and invite Christ into your heart.

It's a life-changing decision. You have nothing to lose, and everything to gain. I'll be praying for you.

Winter Blessings

An Acronym

W – White, crisp, fresh-fallen snow, glistening in the sunlight. Our dog can't resist rolling around in it. We go for winter walks, listen to the snow crunch beneath our feet, and enjoy the beauty. It reminds me that if we choose to follow Jesus, He will wash our sins as white as snow.

I – Ice, clear crystal ornaments in the shape of icicles hanging on the trees, and lacing the edge of the roof of our house. Ice skaters holding hands as they glide over the slick glass. The sound of their skates cutting along the ice. Eventually melting, as God melts the walls of our hearts with the warmth of His love.

N - Nature's beauty. God created each item, so beautiful in its own way. All together making such a masterpiece, expounding to His marvelous greatness and handiwork.

T – Time. To everything there is a season, and a time to every purpose under Heaven. This season is a time of rest. Time to recharge, and prepare for the next phase. God makes everything beautiful in His time.

E – Evergreens, standing tall. Birds nesting in their branches, and rabbits hiding in the shade beneath them. Fields of Christmas trees await to be harvested in celebration of the birth of Christ.

R – Red, crimson cardinals. Bright bursts of color against a backdrop of pure, white snow. Their winter songs resonate in the quiet air, reminding us to prevail; spring is coming. They don't worry about tomorrow and neither should we, God is in control.

Thoughts to ponder: meditating on how God has blessed you this winter; saying a prayer of gratitude.

A Godincidence

Definition: Godincidences are different from coincidences, because they are God-ordained events with a specific purpose or outcome. Being in the right place at the right time, but with God in control.

It was a dry, cold winter's day that was about to become a day I would never forget. While cleaning up after breakfast, I heard a knock at the front door. It was a woman and a teenage boy. She introduced herself and told me that when her son was five, he used to live in my house. There had been a fire, and his birth-mother died, but he and his twelve siblings survived. The children had been split up and adopted; she and the boy were unable to find them. She asked if he could walk around to sort out his memories. With his eyes full of tears, He said his favorite spot to hide was beneath the porch. We talked while he was reminiscing, and had a nice visit.

A few days later, I discovered a gorgeous, bright pink Azalea plant on my porch, with a thank you note attached. I was so surprised and prayed he would find his siblings someday. God works in mysterious ways and I could not have imagined His great plans.

Time passed, and one evening my husband and I were visiting with his cousins at their house. One of his younger cousins had recently gotten married. He introduced us to his wife, Barb. We shared where we were from, and she began to tell us about her twelve brothers and sisters.

My attention sharpened, and I held my breath as I listened. "We had a house fire, our Mom didn't make it out. We were all adopted by different families and some moved away. Everyone of them has been found, except for our youngest brother…"

I could hardly contain my excitement and blurted out, "I may know who he is and I have his address! "

A few weeks later, Barb called and shared with me they had a big family reunion, full of hugs, stories, and pictures. It deeply warmed my heart.

It's moments like this in life, that somehow make the not-so-good things seem a bit better and give us hope. I thank God I was able to see how both sides of this story came together, and that God allowed me to be a part of it. I actually participated in a "Godincidence!"

Sally Labadie is a retired elementary teacher, principal, science instructor, and coordinator of elementary teaching interns in the Department of Education at Michigan State University. She received her Bachelor of Science and Masters degrees at Eastern Michigan University and administrative certification at Michigan State University.

After journaling some of her memories in the classroom, and after retirement from the public schools she published *The Good, The Oops! and the Funny; Events in the Life of a Teacher*. This was followed by a chapter book, *Danger on the Cliffs*. She then concentrated on writing picture books, *Wooster, the Rooster; Tanner's Turtle; The Schoolhouse Mouse,* and *What's Under All Those Leaves,* and *If I Had a Dinosaur*. Memoirs of working at the college level, *And you Thought I Retired*, was written after retiring from Michigan State University. Sally also compiled and published *The History of Bancroft; A Pictorial History of the Town and its People*. She is now working on another picture book, *The Story of Honk, the Goose*.

Sally grew up in Carleton, Michigan but moved to Bancroft with her husband, Harold, where they operated the Love Funeral Home for forty years. She continues to write memoirs of her life.

Sally Labadie

The Downs and Ups of Learning to Walk in Snowshoes

2001

What happens when you get more than a foot of snow, then more snow that blows into drifts of several feet, and then more accumulation over two weeks? Does cabin fever set in?

Last week I borrowed a neighbor's snowshoes. I think he knows how I like to be outdoors. He told me that he doesn't use them anymore, and that I was welcome to them. It didn't take long to get the old wooden frames over my boots and fasten the straps tight. In my first attempt, I walked around our yard and then went to the village well house that sits at the front of a twenty acre field behind my home, and back. I only fell once, when I put one snowshoe on top of the other.

For more practice I went on several longer walks to the woods behind the well house and back. To move on snowshoes is a totally different walking experience. The challenge is to learn how to walk as normal as possible while keeping your feet apart…yeah, right! You sink down a few inches as a rule, but the webbing keeps you from going through the snow as a boot would. Dressing so you don't get too warm seems a challenge. Your face gets cold, but you work up a sweat.

One day came when the sun begged me to get out and play. I strapped on the wooden shoes and headed out back. I saw the deer, mice and rabbits had been well fed. Someone had put food on the edge of the service drive to the well house, but after the last snow the plow had covered the animals' food. This did not deter the hungry critters. They had dug into the pile of goodies and pieces of food were littered in the snow, along with those visible and ever present rabbit pellets. Deer and rabbit tracks were thick in the area.

The air was crisp and stung my nostrils, and I breathed heavily with the cold. I trudged through a wooded area where long grasses usually grow among the trees. The shoes made it difficult to step over fallen branches that were covered by snow. Since I didn't have poles to help me, I grabbed a few trees for stability until I noticed a nice stand of poison ivy on one tree I had just touched. While the vines were dried and appeared dead, I knew that the oils are ever present. I was glad I had heavy gloves on. The going was tough, and even tougher when I hit an air pocket and fell. I floundered in the snow trying to get up, which caused me to sink deeper. I finally got one snowshoe up, put my weight on it, and with my left hand worked my left foot out of the screwed up position I was in. I stumbled up and out of the woods until I reached the solid ground of the field.

I brushed the snow off, shook it out of my gloves, and was thankful that the stumbling took place behind a grove of pines so I couldn't be seen from the road. I retraced my tracks back to the garage where I sat on a low stool, took off the snowshoes, and hung them on a hook to dry.

I returned those snowshoes to my neighbor in the spring, and decided that when we have another winter of soft, deep snow, I would buy my own. That time didn't come until 2011 when we had moved a mile south on a gravel road. I now had 100 acres of woods and farm fields to explore in all seasons.

Those early experiences may have dampened my clothing and put me into a stand of poison ivy, but it didn't dampen my desire to try snowshoeing again. My husband, Harold, wasn't too happy. He said I'd probably break a leg, but isn't snow soft enough to prevent a broken bone?

Heedless of his warning, I headed to the sporting goods to buy my own snowshoes. It was late in the season…early February, and most stores were either all out of them, or they were priced too high for me. I got a lucky break and found a pair on sale at an East Lansing store that came with a storage bag and trekking poles. I was eager to try them out. With the snow piled over a foot deep, for practice I would go slowly and head to the nearby pasture to feed the neighbor's horses.

After cutting up apples and carrots, I adjusted the trekking poles, but they didn't feel firm. Well, I decided that maybe they are supposed to have a little give. I sat down in the garage, strapped on the new snowshoes and headed out. Oops! The snow was soft, so I sunk in pretty deep. I thought they were supposed to let me walk ON the snow! With the poles to help me stay steady, a bag of goodies around my right wrist, and determination in my mind, I trekked out across our yard.

Whoops! I wasn't keeping my feet far enough apart and kept putting one foot over the back of the snowshoe of my other foot. You have to pick up your feet and place them away from the other one. Oh-oh, I did it again, falling forward on my knees. The poles helped me get up…clumsily, but up. How do you stand up with the snowshoes crossing each other? With the pasture gate in sight, I again misplaced a foot and went down. As I used the poles to help me stand up, the left one came apart. I struggled to coordinate my feet and hands to figure how to stand, and picked up the pieces of the pole. I tried to put it together without success, so I just put both poles in one hand and trudged the rest of the way without using them.

By that time two of the horses weren't sure what was going on and were running back and forth across the pasture. Once I was at the gate in an upright position, they calmed down and approached me and eagerly chomped on their treats. I saw the neighbor had a path cleared from the gate to his house, so I followed it to his porch and tried to fix the pole. He came out and tried to help me, but a piece of the pole was missing. I returned to the spot where I had fallen. Nothing. Surely, it would be sticking out of the snow. I decided I'd follow my tracks back home, take off the snowshoes and return to look more closely without them.

After that second examination of the area, I found nothing. I went back home and tried to fit the poles together. I loosened one of the plastic parts that went around the pole, and the missing piece slid out and onto the floor. Duh! I fixed the pole, put them and the snowshoes up to dry and called it quits for the day.

Several days later it was time for another excursion. I put the shoes on and headed for the woods when a cold wind hit my face like icicles. I decided I would walk another day, and returned to the warmth of the house. The weather report said it would warm up on the weekend. Yes! That would be my next goal.

Saturday came and I eagerly dressed for the trek. The snow had settled and the surface was a little crustier, so my feet didn't sink in as much. I walked all the way to the back entrance to the woods without much trouble with the poles…that is, except one again started to "give" as if it wasn't tight enough. I stopped, did my best to tighten it, and started again. I only crossed my feet a couple times, but managed to right them without stumbling.

I wondered, however, how am I supposed to hold my hands on the poles? They have loops to put around your wrist to keep from dropping them, but should I put my hands over the tops? That's what I had been doing. It seemed awkward, and caused my weight to push the poles into the snow. Thinking about skiers and how they hold their poles, I imitated that. It worked. The poles were not there to support my weight, but only to help me balance. They did so by lightly touching the snow. I crossed the first field without a problem.

As I started across a second field, I stopped to rest, when the snow started to fall thick and fast. A layer of the white fluff covered my coat in mere minutes, and I looked like a snowperson. All I would need was a carrot for a nose, I thought. I glanced back at where I had come from, and wondered if I should go back that way or cross this field that leads to the country road. I decided on the road. I was working up a sweat and a thought crossed my mind. It's no wonder skiers don't wear heavy clothes. As I worked my way across the field, I became so warm the snow on my coat had melted and the new snow was melting as soon as it landed on me.

Finally! The road! It had been plowed and had only a thin layer of packed snow on it. The falling snow had tapered off to only a few flakes fluttering down, so it would be easy to navigate. Hmmm. Do I take the snowshoes off or keep them on, I wondered? I didn't see a stump near the road that I could sit on to unfasten them, so I kept up the pace with them on. It was easy to shuffle along this time, with no snow to sink into. I went around the bend in the road when the sound of someone walking behind me broke the cold silence. A neighbor came up beside me, walking his tiny Jack Russell terrier. After we exchanged a few words, he walked on ahead of me and I continued shuffling. I decided it would be easier to walk on the packed snow without the snowshoes. I made sure no cars were coming, bent down, unfastened the shoes and carried them the rest of the way home.

I hope I will get better at this soon.

And Harold, I haven't broken a leg yet!

The Greening of December

1998

The past few years, instead of the usual rush of snow and frigid temperatures, winter has crept in slowly and brought only light amounts of snow. This past November ushered in a strange December...one that scientists have been warning us about for some time.

This year, Thanksgiving came with mild weather. While on a family holiday at my sister Wendy's in Ypsilanti, we took the children out to play while wearing light jackets. At school the students resorted to sweaters and hoodies, and few gloves and hats were seen.

On November 30, the temperature was in the high 50s. All afternoon the rain slowly drizzled and soaked the ground. As I arrived home from work late that night, worms had crawled across the driveway, and Harold, my husband, mentioned that he had seen a frog in the yard.

The following days were the same. The sun shone, the kids played outside and parents put off buying boots and gloves. At night Harold counted over 120 geese on our pond. The corn had been picked, leaving only stubble in the rows, so deer had few places to hide. Five deer; four bucks and a doe were taken by lucky hunters out of our woods during the hunting season, more than ever before.

On Friday, December 4, the fog rolled in and school was delayed for two hours. It was foggy all afternoon, and became thicker during the night. The next morning it started to clear and left everything wet, as if there had been a rainstorm.

On Saturday afternoon I again headed for Ypsilanti. There was an abnormal temperature, 59 degrees before noon. I went into my mother's backyard, where she had mums in full bloom, and several new, beautiful, wide open roses. I expect late blossoms in September, and sometimes early October…but December?

As I drove Mother to the shopping center, I heard a noise from birds in the trees lining Ellsworth Road. There was a mass of birds overhead, as if they were flocking for migration. The grackles were either late for leaving or early to return.

If this unseasonable weather continues, we may need to be mowing grass instead of shoveling snow, and Santa will need to attach wheels to the rudders on his sleigh.

Global warming? Hmm. Could the scientists be correct?

Patti Rae Fletcher discovered her passion for writing while being employed in an elementary school library for fifteen years. She graduated from the Children's Institute of Literature and attends several writing conferences annually. She has written for *Scholastic Book Fairs, Family, Fish, and Game* magazine, *Jack and Jill, Woman's World,* and *Downriver and Grosse Ile Dprofile* along with several other publications online and off.

Fletcher's book, *This Sign Was Mine, Message Received!,* is a short memoir of her experiences of how she has received signs, synchronicities, and love from the Universe. She interpreted these life changing messages and wants to help others do the same. Patti believes every human is given ethereal life guidance throughout their lives.

Presently, Fletcher is the Vice President of the Shiawassee Area Writers group. She has two picture books almost complete, one creative non-fiction about a nymph, and the other about a leprechaun with a special condition. The sequel to her previous book is expected in 2019. This will include more experiences about spiritual signs and how to recognize them.

Patti lives in lower east Michigan with her husband. She enjoys being with family, friends, fishing, boating, hiking, traveling, and being in nature as much as possible.

For updates on new releases, follow Patti at www.pattiraefletcher.com or like her Facebook page: This Sign Was Mine at pattiraefletcher

The Snow Heart

Thirty years of being the best mother, wife, and caregiver I could possibly be has defined who I am, or at least that's what I used to think.

Since my children have moved on to their own lives, my husband a self-sufficient man, and my mother, coupled with the fact that my best friend and my biggest fan -my mother- passed away in 2010, I had begun to feel I no longer made a difference in anyone's life or in mine. I felt lost and not needed. That feeling didn't last long, because I soon became consumed by days, weeks, and months of caregiving for my wonderful, soft spoken, easy-going father. A hero in my eyes.

This is the man who taught me how to hunt slimy night-crawlers, bait my hook, reel in fish, clean and cook them by the time I was ten. He was also my first dance partner, and no one had to tell me he was the most handsome man in the entire world. After my mom passed, I took care of him for almost three years, doing whatever needed to be done. There were bills to pay, meals to prepare, doctor's appointments to schedule and home care visits. I made it my full-time mission to coax a smile from Dad each and every day to keep his spirit positive. This kept me from going into that dark pit after my mom's death. Dad's mind was good up to our final visit. He never missed an opportunity to give me a kiss in gratitude for all that I did for him each day, but internally he was a mess. His body couldn't carry on past February 2013.

The day before Dad's funeral was the day it hit me. Total annihilation. I had lost my mother and realized I hadn't accepted or grieved her death, and now Dad was gone too. How would I survive and would I want to? I couldn't do the funeral thing again. My thought was, I wouldn't go. In reality, I knew that wasn't an option. Everything was set for the funeral. The service would be identical to my mother's. A five hour viewing one day. The picture boards were done, announcements printed, services set, and no procession. There was nothing to keep my mind or body busy. I knew the funeral would be just right but what about all the past discussions and decisions and all those unanswered questions. How could I believe they didn't really die, and they were still with me? Were they really together now? How would I go on?

My husband had to run into work for a few hours leaving me alone to my agonizing thoughts, doubts, devastation and unanswered questions. I became overwhelmed to the point of sobbing and screaming into the air for answers, from somewhere, from someone. I forced myself to take a few deep breaths and then decided maybe a long walk would clear my mind, and uplift my spirit, although I had doubts anything could work.

The weather was bitter cold, but not enough to freeze the free flow of constant tears that I didn't seem to have any control over. I allowed them to fall from my face. They slid from the bottom of my cheeks, onto my coat and then rolled down to the earth. I trudged along with my head low; my body felt as though it was filled with concrete and lead, each step taking such effort.

I don't remember how long I'd walked when I stopped at a corner to blow my nose. I raised my eyes as several beams of the sun shone through a tiny break in the gray dreary clouds that shadowed the day and my heart. The rays landed upon a rooftop across the street and to my disbelief there was a ten-foot snow heart. The snow around the heart had melted revealing the black shingles. The heart shape glistened and twinkled on the roof like the reflection of the sun's rays upon ripples over the water's surface, so bright it hurt to focus on them. All I could think was, wow!

A shudder traveled through my body. A sound escaped through my lips that resembled a throaty laugh despite the tears still wet on my face and my inner devastation. I glanced around thinking this brilliant light show surely would have attracted an audience. I stood transfixed as I marveled at a house top in front of me. It was the most well known symbol of love of all time. And here it was, right before my eyes and suddenly I just knew. It was a sign that had been singled out for me, only me on this day. It was meant to show up at this moment in my desperation and immeasurable woefulness.

The tears stopped; my shoulders lifted. As I stood with my face to the sky, tranquility, warmth, and love replaced the frigid wind and the nerves that had twitched through my exhausted body moments before. It felt as if the Universe had wrapped me in a hot blanket, straight out of the dryer. I stared for what seemed a long while, probably only minutes, but at that moment, there was no doubt I would make it through this day, and Dad's funeral the next day, and the next, and eventually the rest of my life.

Tomorrow, family and friends would gather to say their final so longs to an extraordinary man, a man I'd been lucky enough to call Dad for all my life.

The message of the snow heart was vibrant and clear. Heart shapes have always represented love, and this one, without exception, was with a capital L. The moment I saw the rooftop heart and felt what I felt, I knew this had to be an ethereal experience. It wasn't the perfect shape or sight, but it was the strength, hope, and power I felt within those moments.

I knew I was not alone, despite the wrenched feeling in my soul. It was on this corner I stood like a statue and felt more love circulate through my being than I'd ever known, and I've been blessed with a lot of love in my life. The inner warmth, the slight tremble, and the vivid visions that raced across my thoughts were about all the lives that were touched by my dad in his tender generous ways while he lived his eighty-four years on earth. I felt a sense of complete unexpected calm where just moments ago I was a vibrating mass of tears, twitches, and nerves.

My vision encompassed specific relatives, friends, and neighbors who were also grieved by my dad and the earthly loss. I had forgotten that even though I am an only child, I wasn't alone in my sorrow. Many people cared for and loved my dad, but they loved me as well. And I could feel it, right there and then, on that street corner. Before I left I snapped a photograph of the rooftop with the love sign. My husband and I drove by that house a couple of hours later and the snow heart was gone. Had anyone else seen the snow heart?

Since this day I see heart shapes in various places. Some people even call me, *The heart lady*. I see them when I slice open fruits and vegetables, within the fur of animals, in the sky, on pavement, on tree bark, in heart shaped leaves, reflections, and even on my body. I'm reminded with every heart shape sighting of its message, its message of love, that I am loved, and to always share that love with others, for we never know anyone's adversities, where they've been, what they're going through, and what lies ahead.

There are days I wake up with a particular thought or question on my mind, and I struggle for an answer. Before long, sometime throughout the day I'll know without a doubt the answer, when I see a heart shape and I always do. I'll feel the same sensations of love that I had felt that day on the corner only not as intense. The sensation directs me to the answer. It can be a yes, or no or I take it as, *you're on the right path, keep on going*, kind of answer.

Heart shapes are the strongest of my signs since my parent's transition, but they are not the only signs I've received. My life, my beliefs, thoughts, and experiences will never be the same. I'm not the same. I now know I have reasons to be here. I know and accept my strengths and weaknesses. I now understand my purpose more than ever before.

I have encountered situations and phenomenons that are almost unbelievable. This story is based on chapter six of *This Sign Was Mine! Message Received!* My memoir contains photographs I snapped myself and eleven other stories of synchronicities, Universe or spiritual signs, and their messages.

I believe everyone is given signs to help them through this life's journey. I think we brush off coincidences when we should contemplate what we were thinking at the time, or any ongoing questions that continue to pop into our thoughts.

Maybe you remember a time in your life you've felt a complete unexpected, unexplained calm or knowing at the most unlikely of times. Have you seen or felt any signs? Have you asked? Are you open to receive?

My wish for you is to know you are forever loved, never alone, and that you are able to always find that special place of peace and happiness within your mind, body, and soul. Breathe. Be silent. Listen.

Here I Am
(Two person poem)

(In remembrance of my mother 1933-2010. Begins before my birth)

"When asked to share a favorite Christmas story at a Woman's Church United Group meeting, my first thought was of a children's book, *Rocking Horse Christmas* by Mary Pope Osborne. However, after I had made that decision, I wrote these words the evening before the meeting. The words flowed onto a notepad. I felt a strong internal nudge to share this poem with the group and now with you in this book. No doubt, my best friend, biggest fan, and inspiration came through my mom on this poem."

(Mom)

Where are you baby of mine

Nine years is a long long time

Maybe a baby isn't meant to be

I'm still grateful for my husband and me

(Me)

Here I am, spirit from above singing you a song

Don't weep Mother-God's timing is never wrong

I will be there soon wait and see

He has promised a March delivery

(Mom)

Where are you baby of mine

In my arms you'd be divine

Another long year has passed

365 days I've asked

(Me)

Here I am, born this March day

Now we can snuggle, kiss, and play

I tried to tell you have no fears

We'll make up for all nine years

(Mom)

My doubt perished the moment you were born

Five pounds of precious infant for me to adorn

We'll plan parties, play games, and have girls' nights out

Together we will learn **love** is what life is all about

(Me)

Here I am, all grown up today

With two sons and a granddaughter in ballet

How quickly time disappears

It's been over fifty years

(Mom)

My baby you are the best thing in my life

Now you are a mother, grandmother, and wife

In the mirror an old gray-haired lady I see

But inside I know that's not the real me

(Me)

Here I am, when did all the years drift away

I have multiple memories on instant replay

Fishing, family, friends, dances and so much laughter

You and Dad are the best at happily-ever-after

(Mom)

What matters is all we have done to this date

It's the sharing, caring, and love that carries weight

Memories will come when needed most

Heaven's angels have always been close

(Me)

Here I am, I tried to make you proud of me

I never felt good enough-you didn't agree

A strong mother I can't imagine without

You'd be with me forever I had no doubt

(Mom)

I will always be with you-have no fears

Eternity is more than any sum of years

When the clock chimes and I'm called home

God and I will never leave you alone

(Me)

Here I am, without you-how will I get along

You've encouraged, inspired, and kept me strong

I will especially miss our daily chats

Your practical jokes and talks about democrats

(Mom)

You must go within praise God for life and humankind

Our minds and souls have been *forever* intertwined

I'll be there on time-you wait and see

Through meditation you'll know it's me

(Me)

Here I am, with eyes closed-I inhale exhale-there're golden rays

Our kin who are able join with our love and unspoken praise

I can almost smell the ham and your favorite the roasted turkey

And there's Dad still famous for his Christmas sausage and venison jerky

(Mom)

Here I am! Merry Christmas baby of mine

(Me)

Here I am! Merry Christmas Mom-right on time

Pattie Rae Fletcher

The Perfect Place to Ponder
Detroit River
(10 syllable lines)

Ice floes crack and creak at the fishing dock
The gulls scatter at the crunch of my steps
Freeze or flow-what will the river decide
A winter haze stands like a barricade
Not rain nor snow but somewhere in-between
In the gray distance a freighter's horn blasts
The echo lingers my neck hairs quiver
Surrounded within this heavy vapor
Entranced in this oppressive atmosphere
The floes compare to an ancient mural
Shattered remnants knifelike jagged edges
Others are as polished as tumbled stones
None the same-vast to sparse and thick to thin
I grin as ducks land and secure a lift
Parallel marks merge on frozen pieces
Who spun their wheels was it frolic or rage
Like life some bits are crystal clear and smooth
Other parts are ragged rough and broken
A few know their heart's journey from the start
Others bump and twist in their endless search
Many slabs meld and travel in tandem
Hang on tight there's a better place ahead
The current travels at a rapid pace
Delivering the floes to the Great Lakes
Weeks ago the river solidified
Nature's fragments will soon unite again

Winters mist opaque-what's coming my way
As in the future it's a mystery
Breathe in release and let the breath exclaim
I am in the splendor of the present
And this is the perfect place to ponder . . .

L.K.Perry currently lives in Swartz Creek, Michigan where she grew up. Perry is an active member of the Swartz Creek United Methodist church. She moved back to her childhood city in 2014 to help her brother take care of their aging Mother. Perry has an Associate's Degree in Liberal Arts received with honors, Phi Theta Kappa. Her studies included Literature, Poetry, Creative Writing, and Language. Perry's memoir *Evergreen* is to debut in this anthology *Winter in the Mitten* compiled by Shiawassee Area Writers (SAW). Perry is a member and the treasurer of SAW.

L.K. Perry

Evergreen

I love Christmas time, but this year I struggled to enjoy the festivities. Surrounded by the holiday spirit, I just couldn't get into the season's joy.

Fresh evergreen trees for sale at my church reminded me of my childhood Christmas days. Every year I would pile into the family car with my siblings and parents as we headed out to a local tree farm. We enjoyed Christmas light displays along the way. We looked forward to visiting the big barn building which contained warm donuts made inside where you could watch the process. Cider was sold by the glass or jug. Dad would buy us a donut and glass of cider before we searched for our tree. Musicians played and sang near an inside fire that produced some warmth in the drafty setting. As we gathered around with our treats, we sang along.

Once let loose in the field, my parents found it a challenge to keep us all together. Looking for a tall, full, well-shaped blue spruce, when we thought we found one, we would holler, "Over here! Over here!" Dad carried the saw provided by the owner. Once we all agreed on the tree, Dad would cut it down. After it was strapped to the car, Dad bought a jug of cider and a dozen assorted donuts which consisted of cinnamon, powder, and plain. Then we headed home to decorate our tree. Dad hung the lights and garland. Mom helped us kids hang the ornaments and tinsel. After we finished, we would turn off all the lights except the ones on the tree. Beaming with love and pride, the beauty of the tree shone in our eyes and melted our hearts.

My father loved Christmas. He died when I was thirteen. This was one of my favorite family traditions. I hadn't thought about it in years.

. . .

Inside the United Methodist church, a twenty-foot tree stood in the sanctuary near the altar, adorned in festive array. Banners, proclaiming faith, love, joy, peace, and hope hung under evergreen garland, highlighting a side wall. An evergreen wreath sat regally on the altar. I thought about how the circle represented eternal life with no beginning or end.

I had moved back to my childhood neighborhood four years ago to help my aging mother. I joined the church of my youth.

Mom was having some minor issues at that time. She had high blood pressure and a lot of anxiety about her condition. Whenever she saw a blood pressure machine, she would have a panic attack. Her doctor insisted that someone needed to take a reading several times a day. She lived with my brother and he struggled with the attacks. He constantly called me and I drove over two hundred miles every weekend. Finally, I decided to retire early and moved within walking distance from where they lived. After I was able to help mom relax, I got a part-time job and became very involved at my church. Things were running along well until last summer.

Mom was hospitalized with a urinary tract infection. It made her crazy. She kept taking her clothes off, wouldn't stay in bed, and fought with the nurses. After the infection cleared up, they sent her home. Unfortunately she was still acting crazy. She cut the window screen and ran away. At ninety, she managed to escape every deterrent we put in place. We called the police three times. One time, they had to use a police dog to track her.

My brother and I sought help. We made many phone calls and talked to umpteen professionals. We were referred to many people and places that were not able to help us. We didn't qualify for one reason or another. We didn't have enough money for assisted living or even home care assistance. Mom was hallucinating and extremely paranoid. She didn't qualify for a nursing home because she didn't need physical rehabilitation. She had an unbelievable amount of debt which didn't help matters. My brother and I decided that I would manage her money since I had worked fifteen years in financial institutions.

Finally, a geriatric doctor diagnosed her with Alzheimer's and put her on some medication that calmed her down. It took several months for the meds to take effect. In the meantime, she tore her feet up, injured her shoulder, and her blood pressure got all out of whack again.

With five different doctors and multiple appointments, sometimes two or three a week, I was worn out. I guess I shouldn't have been surprised that I wasn't in the Christmas spirit. My spirit was soon to be revived by three events in four days and the calming effect of the holiday's evergreen.

. . .

The first event was a Christmas tea at my church. When asked to buy a ticket, I said, "Thank you for asking, but funds are tight. I'll make an effort to join you next year." Funds were scarce, but it was just an excuse. I hadn't eaten sweets in seven weeks and I didn't want to be tempted. While researching Alzheimer's, several sources suggested sugar increased one's probability of getting the disease. I didn't want to put my daughter through what I am experiencing with my mother.

Shortly after I refused, a ticket arrived in the mail. Someone wanted me at the Christmas tea, so what was I to do? How could I say no? The evening of the tea, greeters checked us in and took our coats. The entrance had an elegant display of women's items, which included fancy red hats, a wood-carved hand that held gloves with a pearl necklace, purses, earrings, and white roses on a black satin cloth. Draped across the table's edge hung God's special evergreen in a twinkling garland with attached red, lacy bows.

The tea took place in our family life center. Twenty fabulous tables were set up to serve approximately two hundred women. Each setting was unique and designed by the woman hosting that particular table. My table had a single white Amaryllis in a tall vase encircled with babies breath. White china plates with silver tableware resting on white napkins contrasted the red tablecloth. Clear glass cups with painted Santas surrounded by tea lights sparkled and added merriment to the table. Red shiny gift bags with white tissue paper perfectly fluffed and six Ande mints dressed in their evergreen foil laid next to each setting. My mints called out to me. I watched my friends enjoying theirs, so I decided I'd eat just one. I ate all six.

An outside caterer provided a delicious meal. Our waiters turned out to be men from my church. They did an excellent job of making us feel special. When it came time for dessert, I caved again. The hostess of my table, who bought my ticket, also broke a sugar fast she was on.

"It's Christmas," she said as she shrugged her shoulders at me. I agreed. We would just have to get back on track tomorrow. The laughter and conversation at the tea began to lift my spirit. A married couple entertained us with Christmas songs and stories. It was just what I needed.

. . .

The next day I needed to prepare for another event that I had tried to get out of a few weeks earlier. It was my family get-together. My daughter and her family live two hours away. Who knew what the Michigan roads would be like? That was my excuse to them. Mostly, I wanted to spare them my sour mood. Aware of recent events, they understood what troubled me. My granddaughters insisted that they needed to spend time with me. My daughter offered for them to travel my way so that I wouldn't have to worry about the roads.

So, I said, "Yes." What should we do together? My son-in-law suggested Frankenmuth, a Christmas tourist city. I had been there many times at Christmas. Because of the expense, crowds, and extra miles they would have to drive, we decided against it. I had an idea. A place they had never been.

Durand is a city about ten miles from me known for its train station. The two story structure built in 1905 is Chateau Romanesque architecture. A large patio outside with a black ornate fence guards anyone from stepping out on the tracks. On a previous visit, the museum curator shared that many photo shoots have been taken on the patio. People were enamored with the backdrop of the rails. My girls love to take selfies and pictures so I knew they would love this photo opportunity.

In addition, the station featured dozens of decorated Christmas trees to view for free. Businesses, groups, and individuals create unique trees with their own themes. I helped decorate the tree for my writer's group, Shiawassee Area Writers (SAW). *This is what gave me the idea for my family gathering. I wanted them to see this beautiful evergreen and all the others.*

Our tree stood on a worn, wooden desk with a typewriter that appeared to be from the 1950s. Books written by authors of the group rested under the tree on a special book-designed skirt. A nostalgic theme to take viewers back in time was decided by the president of our group. An empty gift box, designed to look like a book, topped SAW's magical tree. Various ornaments which included bulbs with our member's autographs hung from the branches. My granddaughters took several pictures of my bulb which surprised and touched me.

The Durand train station contained a nostalgic railroad museum. The men of my family enjoyed the historical and local information. My daughter and I noticed my granddaughters huddled around a glass case. They seemed to be fascinated by its contents. We had to check it out. It turned out to be a display of hobo codes.

Two circular rooms, one upstairs and the other down, featured at least a dozen trees in each room. In the downstairs room, an old player piano seemed to beg for a quarter to play a Christmas song. We fed it many quarters that day. My daughter, Lisa, and my mom danced in sync. We laughed as we recorded them. An additional room upstairs had more evergreens and a place for Santa to meet children. We took numerous pictures in and around Santa's chair.

Only a few people besides my family enjoyed the station while we celebrated our time together. My son-in-law loved the quiet, peaceful atmosphere. He said, "This is better than Frankenmuth." Memories were created. My girls must have taken a hundred pictures. Precious moments were captured on video. The love and support of my family filled my heart with the Christmas spirit. This would have been enough for me, but there was more to come.

...

The next night, I attended a Christmas gathering with my writer's group. Brenda, a good friend, introduced me to the group last summer when my world turned upside down while caring for my mom. Elizabeth, our president, invited everyone to her home.

I wore a red shirt with "Dear Santa, it's a long story" written in silver cursive across the front. Everyone brought a snack to go along with the wonderful food Elizabeth provided. I chose tortilla chips and salsa still trying to get back on my sugar-free diet. As authors and writers arrived with their goodies, I knew the diet would wait for another day.

After I mingled, I sat near the beautifully decorated evergreen that touched the ceiling. Shadows from the lights made interesting designs on the wall. Patti Rae Fletcher took a seat next to me. My elbow accidentally nudged her. When I apologized, she giggled because she thought I had a secret to share.

"No secret. Bet you are disappointed," I said. We laughed together.

That night, I bought Patti's book, *This Sign Was Mine - Message Received*. Later as I began to read her book, I couldn't put it down. It was so good. After the final page, I realized that I did have a secret to share with her.

Elizabeth asked us to join her in the living room. Bright-eyed and smiling, she shared that she had gotten an idea in the night. She had our full attention. "What if we all wrote a book together? Individual stories compiled collectively. This would be a great project for our group."

She mentioned what a benefit it would be for those of us who hadn't published yet. She went into detail of what it would take for us to do this. Her enthusiasm and excitement became contagious.

I started to think about what I would write. Some were expressing their ideas out loud. One of our children's authors loved the idea. Her comment to me was, "This project is like a Christmas gift to us." It certainly was a gift to me.

I realized that being a part of this group had helped me keep my sanity during this troubled time for me. The writing was cathartic and it has given me a positive goal to focus on. In addition, the people in this group have been fun and easy to be with.

. . .

I don't know why the evergreen caught my attention this year. Fond memories of my father and his love for the Christmas tree had surfaced this season. We had three evergreens in our small yard. Our favorite one was a blue spruce planted close to the house. A picture of me at age four standing next to the baby tree was taken because we were the same height. The tree grew too tall over the years crowding the house and had to be cut down.

Dad and the blue spruce gone, I watched mom's mind slowly slipping away. At times, I was sad and other times, she made me laugh really hard. Her childish nature was quite the character.

As I pondered mom's age and the disease she was battling, I thought about eternity and heaven. Mom has often been afraid to die. We've had many discussions about Jesus and her receiving him as her Savior and Lord. She seemed to struggle with this. Other people, including pastors, have tried to encourage her. I have put my trust in the Lord while I continue to pray for her.

This year, I was so thankful for my family, friends, and God's evergreen. Jesus has been my hope and strength. He has never left me or given up on me. I have always been able to depend on Him to get me through troubled times.

You will go out in joy and be led forth in peace; the mountains and hills will burst into song before you, and all the trees of the field will clap their hands.

Instead of the thornbush will grow the pine tree, and instead of briers the myrtle will grow. This will be for the Lord's renown, for an everlasting sign, which will not be destroyed.

Isaiah 55:12, 13 NIV

Author and speaker, **Laurie Salisbury**, lives in a rambling old farmhouse in the middle of Michigan. She has published four children's chapter books in the He Reigns series, *Reins of Love, Forever Settled in My Heart, Hope County Fair*, and *Rescued Horse-Rescued Hearts*. She is currently working on book five, *The Harness of the Lord*.

Other publications include, *Nothing to Fear*, an infant/toddler picture book based on II Timothy 1:7, and short story Twelve Shopping Days.

Laurie lives with her husband, Larry, three of her children and two small dogs. She has spent her life loving and serving children. She raised nine children, gave a temporary home, love, and direction, to twenty-eight foster children, and served in Children's Ministry for over thirty years.

Find out more about Laurie at www.lauriesalisbury.com or join her on Facebook @lauriesalisburyauthor.

Laurie Salisbury

Bestest Friend

Dear New Friend,

Hi, my name is Maisy. Please don't call me Daisy, I am not a flower. I wish I had a regular name like Sophia or Chloe, but I'm named after my Aunt Maisy. Jake used to be my friend, but that was before I told him that people used to call my aunt, Crazy Maisy. After I told him, he told blabber-mouth Brayden who told the whole second-grade class. Now every time I try something new they call me Crazy Maisy. It's okay though because my very bestest friend never calls me crazy. He says I'm brave.

I told my mom I was bored, so she gave me a brilliant idea. My mom has lots of brilliant ideas. She said I could get a pen-pal. She chose the pen-pal list and I chose you. Now we can be new friends.

Have you ever been in a cast? I've never been in a cast until now. I used to think it might be cool to have a cast for everyone to sign and draw pictures on. I was wrong. Flat out wrong. It is not fun. It's not cool and it's very itchy. So here I am, stuck in this room, in my bed. I have to lay flat on my back while my friends play outside in the snow. They are having Christmas parties and doing stuff without me. I even had my birthday in this stupid cast. I'm eight now. How old are you?

Do you want to know how I got into this cast? Well, I was trying to do a flip trick on the playscape at school. It didn't work out like I thought it would, and I broke my hip. The doctor says it was the worst broken hip he's ever seen! Then I had surgery and came out with the biggest cast I've ever seen. It goes all around my belly under my chest and halfway down my right leg. The rest of it goes down my left leg so that I can only see my toes. But my bestest friend said that it will heal in no time and I'll be back to my old tricks.

I hear my family laughing. They are doing fun stuff without me again. I don't miss my big sister and brothers that much. My mom makes them play board games with me sometimes. But, I got a new baby sister before I got in the cast and they get to play with her all the time. Mom almost never brings her in here. I was in the hospital for two whole weeks and one time a nurse brought another baby into my hospital room when I was missing my baby sister. That was the nice nurse.

I thought getting out of school for a few months would be great. I hate math, and homework is the worst. But one day this wrinkly old lady showed up at our house saying she was my tutor. She is the oldest teacher I have ever had and she smells like Grandpop's old people home. She talks weird too. She talks too slow. It's like she puts a period between every word she says. Last week she got me a thingy to hang from my bed with pockets. It's white with ugly yellow flowers. It looks like my grandma's blanket. She said I could keep my homework and pencils in it but my bestest friend said it would be a great hiding place for my candy and gum.

Being in a cast is almost as boring as sitting in a math class all day, so my mom got me a TV to watch. It isn't hooked up to cable or anything, so I can only watch movies, but it's better than nothing. I watch it after school with my bestest friend.

One time my dad tried to weigh my cast while I was in it! It all happened on Thanksgiving Day. Most days I have to stay in my bedroom. But not Thanksgiving Day. My dad carried me out to the living room so that I could be with the whole family. It is very scary for someone to carry you when your whole body is in a cast. He laid me on the floor on a blanket. Then he got this crazy idea that he could find out how much this big stupid cast weighs. So, he got mom's bathroom scale and picked me up to set me on it, like I was standing up. Don't tell anyone, but I cried because I thought it would hurt me. When I told my bestest friend he said it was okay to cry. A few days later he said I could forgive my dad since everything is okay now and I didn't get broke again.

When December came, I got so scared I would miss Christmas. I could hear my family decorating the tree without me. They rang the bell ornaments and my brother argued with my sister about putting the star on the top of the tree. My mom got a brilliant idea to put a tiny tree in my room. It's nice, but it isn't the same as the big family tree.

Then I went to the doctor and laid on the bed while he talked to my mom about when the cast should come off. He looked at my x-ray and tapped his fingers on a fat yellow folder crammed with papers. He said he was trying to decide if he should do it before Christmas or after. I shouted, before! It worked. Tomorrow is the day. Right on Christmas Eve. I have been in it for two whole months. It feels like two whole years!

Have you ever been scared-excited? I am. I want the cast off, but the doctor said they have to use a saw. He said it was a safe saw for skin, but I don't know if I believe him. He might just say that to all the little kids so we won't cry or anything. My bestest friend said he will come with me. He won't tell anyone if I cry.

My mom says I have to turn the light off and go to sleep now. I hope you will be my friend and write back. I have to talk to my very bestest friend, Jesus, about his birthday party and I want to talk to him about the sawing tomorrow. Merry Christmas.

Love, Maisy

P.S. They sawed the cast off and it didn't even hurt. I will tell you about my peeling skin and crutches the next time I write. I got a new book for Christmas. I'm going to read it with my bestest friend. Bye!

These rhymes were written and submitted by **Victor Eden**. Victor has a love of poetry and rhymes.

He lives in Owosso with his wife and two sons.

Surprise

It snowed last night
In the morning light
The ground is covered white
Though quite a shocking sight
Always a delight
-for children-

First Snow of the Season

Tiny little snowflakes drift past the window pane
The kids are running through the house, driving me insane
"It's snowing out! It's snowing out!" The smallest races past
"It's finally really snowing out! Winter's here at last!"
I shut my eyes to calm myself and try to keep my cool
When running up again he says, "Do you think they'll close the school?"

The Pine

Blue sky
sunshine
snow has fallen
on the pine

Robed it
in a gown of white
Cold kept it there

all through the night

So in the morning
all could see
the splendor
of a simple tree

Christmas Shopping Past

Searching for the perfect gift
was so time consuming
Never moving fast enough
with Christmas ever looming

Find the present, wrap the present
tie it with a bow
I had to keep on pushing
with so little time to go

No time for Christmas laughter
No time for Christmas cheer
It seemed I had less energy
Each and every year

Christmas Shopping Present

All my time I spend online
doing Christmas shopping
Finding deals and Christmas steals

truly keeps me hopping
With kids in school it's the tool
that helps me save more money
but I have to wait when shipping's late
Which really isn't funny

Future Christmas Shopping

I love my 3D-printer
now they're all the rage
I have a vast list of great gifts
page after page
The one thing I don't like though
even if it is fantastic
Everything it makes it seems
has to be of plastic

Electric Santa

Electric cars, electric trains,
electric flying aero planes
Now self driving, flying too
the world's become an electric zoo

Electric windows, electric eyes
electric dolls with electric cries
electric hearts, electric arms
electric people with electric charms

Electric thoughts in electric brains

acting electrically insane
Electric Santa bring this year
more of your electric cheer

Plug us into one big cable
calm our souls, make us stable
and Dear Santa won't you please
bring us more electric ease

Night Skiing

Moonlight
Nightlight
Shining overhead so bright
You can see the mountains white
With snow
Downhill
Using skill
Trying not to take a spill
Heart thumping with the thrill
Aglow

Ski Lodge

I remember in December
the biting cold, the red hot ember
The mountain snow, your face aglow
skiing through the powder snow

A frozen stream, our breaths of steam
sparkling snow in a bright sunbeam

The wood smoke air, a wisp of hair
the rocking of the ski lift chair

So long ago, but falling snow
makes those memories start to glow
It seems I cannot yet forget
the winter day that we first met

The Child

A long time ago
in a place far away
Inside a manger
A small baby lay

A star shone above
with radiant light
And angels sang songs
in robes of pure white

Shepherds came searching
for an angel had said
That here in this stable
He had his bed

In silence the cattle and donkey
did lie
And the small babe lay quiet
with his mother close by

So it began on that

far night of old
And again and again
the story's been told

The point here is this
and I think it's of worth
Were we more like this child
we would have Peace on Earth

Christmas Rant 2004

It's Christmas time 2004
and once again we're still at war
Kids still sit on Santa's lap
asking for commercial crap
Shoppers rush to buy, buy, buy
never understanding why
Through rain and snow, sleet and hail
the postman strives to bring the mail
Christmas cards from far away
that simply say "Happy Holiday!"
Without a word or written line
whether or not folks are fine
Have the holidays turned more crazy
or have I just gotten old and lazy
A child in a manger from a long time ago
now has Christmas trees and snow
With elves and holly and blinking lights
to brighten up those cold Christmas nights
With help from Frosty and Mr. Grinch
Santa brings Christmas, but just in a pinch

There's Rudolph with his bright red nose
to lead the way where ere he goes
And now there is the Polar Express
now maybe I'm wrong, It's just my guess
But I'll bet next year there will be a witch or two
cackling over a Christmas brew
They'll switch Rudolph and Santa's head
and just before the kiddies go to bed
Christmas will be saved and Santa will come
bringing his goodies to everyone
It's interesting how far we can stray
from the stable and manger where the small baby lay
With a single bright star high up above
the only thing He had to bring
~was Love

First Time Sledding

Upon my sled, I sit with dread
facing down the hill
Dad gives a push and with a rush
I'm feeling such a thrill
It's like flying, almost dying
The world is flashing by
Snow whips my face as down I race
My voice lets out a cry
To my sled I cling as my fingers sting
and still my speed increases
As the cold wind chills, my mind is thrilled
and hopes it never ceases
Suddenly though I began to slow

and heaving two big sighs
I do my best and at last
open my eyes

Childhood Challenges

At a spot called, Dead Man's Drop
Now knee deep in snow
Three boys stood as best they could
and surveyed what was below

Atop "The Hill" in the winter's chill
stood Thomas, Jack, and Howard
Standing with their sleds, they crooked their heads
and looked what seemed straight downwards

An icy glaze from a morning haze
had made the climbing slow
And the sparkling scene with its brilliant sheen
would set most hearts aglow

But on the crown and looking down
their view was much more different
Their braggadocio had gotten low
their words less effervescent

Foot to crown, almost straight down,
the mammoth hillside canted
From the top their eyeballs popped
the way the whole thing slanted

Victor Eden

"Not so bad," said one brave lad
looking down his nose
His voice was soft for the edge dropped off
not too far from his toes

They were three amigos, where ever he goes we goes
and they thought they could conquer Dead Man's Hill
But on that spot there at the top
going down had lost its thrill

They were thinking Georgie Sprout
who ran it just last year
Just by chance a hanging branch
almost took off his ear

The year before Axol Dorr
ran into a tree
Like hitting a boulder, he broke his shoulder
and fractured his left knee

But Carl Brown, he went down
backward on a dare
years ago after one big snow
It's said he made it, fair and square

The list went on. Howard, Jack and Tom
knew the tales by heart
From school yard chums and street corner bums
they heard the legends start

But it had gotten late and they would wait
to tame that tiger's wile

Another year they might face their fear
and ride it down in style.

So they turned around to head back down
still just sledding rookies
At that stage of life where internal strife
could be fixed with milk and cookies

Jason Bullard is a graduate from Long Ridge Writers Group. He has written a short story called *The Long Walk* in the *Storyteller* magazine January 2015 issue. His debut book of short stories is called *Strange Tales Book One*. He enjoys writing everyday and reads as much as possible. His passion for creative writing began at an early age. He likes to write fiction that deals with thriller, horror, mystery, and some science fiction. Jason has a website *bullard.xyz*. Contact him at his email *jasonbullard41@gmail.com*. Jason lives in Michigan in a small town called a Owosso.

Christmas Reunion

The Lane Estate in northern Michigan stood one and a half miles from the main road. A huge metal gate with a security code separated the house from civilization. They knew how to decorate for Christmas. All their windows had lights and the pine trees on the grounds were adorned in color. They got wealthy from the oil industry and had companies of their own. They lived in expensive houses and drove brand new cars. Charles Lane, the father, lived in the house with his nurse Ann Edwards. His five children were grown. It was Christmas Eve and he wanted his family home.

Curtis Lane, the oldest child, drove up to the metal gate. He rolled down the window on his old Chevy truck. The strong, north breeze blew tendrils of his brown hair. He punched in the security code and the metal gate opened with a creaking sound. He cringed at the sound; it reminded him of a teacher putting their nails across a chalkboard. He rolled up his window and drove down the long driveway. He noticed on the windshield that the snow was coming down harder.

Curtis disliked snow, that is why he moved to the west to stay in the heat. He could remember being close to his dad. As he got older he had different dreams. They fought about it until one day he just left. It had been so long ago.

As the mansion came in view to Curtis it looked just as it did on the day he left. He pulled up the circle drive and parked behind a vehicle. He gripped the steering wheel tight, closing his eyes. When he opened his eyes he saw his younger brother, Billy, getting out of his car. He smiled, hurried out of his truck to greet his brother.

"Billy, it has been too long. How are you?"

Billy turned around and smiled, "My brother, yes it has been too long. I'm good. I am surprised you recognize me."

Curtis laughed. "How could I forget that bright red hair of yours."

They both laughed and hugged. Curtis was happy that he saw Billy first. They always got along well and as boys stuck up for one another.

Billy laughed. "I had to bring Lucy, Susan, and her husband, Chad, with me. My blazer was the only vehicle with enough room."

"How was your drive here?"

"It was chaos. I had to pick up Susan and her husband at the airport. I then had to pick up Lucy at the bus station. It was crazy."

They both laughed and started toward the front door. The door was dark wood with a big knocker set in the center. Billy opened the door without knocking and they both stepped into the front hall. Curtis noticed the hall was all decorated with garland and lights. The atmosphere was warm and pleasant. Curtis' childhood memories came back.

He saw the staircase, remembering all the times he had ran down it. To his right, Curtis could see the living room and on his left was his dad's office. His dad spent most of his time in the office throughout their childhood. He remembered all the different rooms throughout the house.

The memories were so strong that a single tear ran down his cheek. He quickly rubbed it away before his brother noticed. Loud voices came from the hall on the left side of the staircase. Voices were coming from the den. As the two got closer they looked in the den, to find their sisters Lucy and Susan. Their brother James was talking to Chad.

Curtis felt overwhelmed with emotions once again. Tears filled his eyes. His heart skipped a beat and a warm sensation covered his body. He had a lump in his throat, he cleared his throat. This made everyone in the den turn toward him. There were smiles all around as they saw Curtis in the doorway.

They welcomed him in the den with a drink. It had been a long time since he saw any of them. He ran his own business called Taco Wave, a bunch of food trucks on the west coast. It was a change for him to go from the weather in Michigan to the warmth of California.

The family, having a great time in the den turned on some music and became reacquainted. It definitely had been a long time and Curtis was happy to catch up with his siblings. He was glad that no one brought up what happened in the past with him and his father.

Nurse Edwards stood in the doorway of the den several minutes before she spoke in a low deep tone, "Dinner is ready."

They all looked at the nurse without saying a word, the music still played in the background. Curtis was afraid to move or even speak. As the group entered the dining room the table was ready for guests. They walked around the big table to their seats. Curtis sat next to Billy and Lucy. He wanted to be close to his dad and look into his eyes.

They didn't have to wait long for their father. Nurse Edward pushed their father to the table, his wheelchair nudged the edge jostling their water goblets.

Charles Lane cleared his throat and spoke softly, "I am glad you could all make it. I would also like to say a prayer for my beloved wife Martha who couldn't be here."

Curtis was in tears over his dad's prayer. He also noticed that he was not aging well. His dad used to have thick dark hair, now it was snow white and had become thinner. His once smooth face now was dry and rough looking with creases and deep wrinkles. Curtis wondered what his brothers and sisters thought about their father's appearance. No one seemed shocked as each sibling began eating.

Curtis got up and ran to his father's side. Charles was tipping over in his wheelchair. Curtis was just a few seconds too late as his father hit the floor. He rolled his father over on his back. Charles' face a pasty white, he still was choking and you could hear him wheezing.

"Someone, help him. He is still choking," cried Curtis through tears.

The others jumped to aid Curtis. Susan's husband, Chad, was the first one to help. They tried to stop the choking by hitting his back, but that didn't work.

Charles' eyes started to bulge and his lips were blue. Charles managed to whisper one word to Curtis. It sounded like "key." Curtis heard the word and for a brief moment was confused and saw his father stop breathing. He fell on top of his father crying so bad that his whole body shook out of control. Curtis watched his father gradually give up his life.

The rest of them were crying and speechless. The sniffles could be heard throughout the room. Curtis cried so loud it echoed off the walls.

James was first to speak, "What happened to the nurse?"

Everyone looked around the room in shock. In all the commotion no one even realized the nurse was missing. A scream broke out shattering the silence. Curtis was the last to leave as he closed his father's eyes with his hand.

James entered the den. He was followed by Curtis who passed the others. They both heard what Nurse Edwards said to Lucy about killing their father. James angrily charged at Nurse Edwards. Curtis was just too slow to grab his arm. James never saw the knife until she stabbed it in his neck. James hit the floor holding his neck as blood oozed from the wound. She was about to stab James again but Curtis knocked her down by tackling her.

Nurse Edwards had a shocked look on her face. She spoke in a low tone, "I am so sick of you kids. I was sick of your father; he left me out of his will. I took care of him all these years, changing his diapers, making sure he got to the doctor and being there when you kids were off doing whatever."

Nurse Edwards ran at Curtis but he was too fast for her. She just missed him with the knife. She saw the others standing by the door. She didn't hesitate as she ran toward them. Chad stood in front of Susan to protect her. Billy wasn't as lucky as he turned to flee as Nurse Edwards drove the knife in his back. Billy screamed as he hit the floor. Nurse

Edwards couldn't get the knife free from Billy's back so she left it there. She ran down the hall toward the front door.

Curtis stood up watching the chaos unfold in front of him. As he watched Nurse Edwards flee, he walked over to James...he never had a chance. He then walked over to Lucy who was barely breathing and he didn't dare move her. He noticed Chad kneeling down next to Billy. He went over to them hoping Billy would be fine.

As Curtis got closer, he saw the blade of the knife was completely buried in his back. He wanted to get Nurse Edwards and he ran toward the front door. Curtis noticed Nurse Edwards was trying to get the front door opened but her bloody hands kept slipping on the door knob. She just got the door opened right before he got there. She ran out of the house into the snowstorm. Curtis stopped at the door, he could barely see through the snow. He didn't know where she went; it was like the snow swallowed her up. A wireless phone was on a stand; he picked it up and dialed 911. An operator came on but before she could say more he told her everything that happened. The phone went dead, Curtis hit the talk button several times but there was no dial tone. He then remembered that he left his cell phone in his truck and was about to get it when he heard a clicking sound.

"I am sorry, Curtis. I can't let you leave," said Chad.

Curtis turned around to see Chad holding a pistol and aiming it at him. He asked in a concerned voice, "Why are you doing this? We need to get help."

"There is no need for that now."

"What do you mean?"

As if on cue, Susan appeared. She came to Chad, putting her hand on his shoulder. She spoke in an unemotional voice, "I took care of her. Is this our only loose end?"

"No, the nurse got away."

Susan had a shocked look on her face. She looked at Curtis then at Chad. She asked, "Did you ask him what Father said?"

"No, I was about to."

Susan pulled a small pistol from her back, pointed it at Chad's head and pulled the trigger. Chad's body crumpled to the floor. Susan then pointed the pistol at Curtis. Curtis more confused than scared raised his hands.

"Brother, I don't want to hurt you. I just want to know what Father told you."

Curtis smiled, now he understood his father's last words. He would never tell her, having the advantage, he would never tell her. Susan saw him smiling and shot a warning shot. She was getting angrier; she aimed the gun at his leg. She was about to pull the trigger when something from behind hit her in the head.

Lucy stood over Susan with red marks on her throat. She wasn't dead like Susan had thought; she'd just pretended to be dead. Lucy dropped the bat and came over to Curtis. She gave her brother a hug and began crying on his shoulder. In the distance they could hear sirens, Curtis went over by the wall to hit the button to open up the gate. He was hoping the snow wouldn't slow them down. He found Lucy's coat and covered her up. They both walked onto the front porch to wait for the police.

It took the police a few hours to get it all sorted out. Susan was arrested and there was an APB for Nurse Edwards. The police said she couldn't have gotten too far and they would find her. Lucy went to the hospital and Curtis told her he would meet her there.

Curtis wandered to the library. He was looking for a certain book. The book was "Treasure Island. His father used to read it to him. He removed the book and found the key inside. The key was brass and as big as a skeleton key. He held the key up in the air and turned it around a few times. Curtis heard the grandfather clock strike one, it was already Christmas. He knew that this would be a Christmas he would never forget, putting the key in his pocket hoping the key would be worth it since it cost him his family. He got in his car and headed toward the hospital. A single thought went through Curtis' head, love of money is the root of evil.

Douglas Cornell writes fiction, ranging from adventure stories to the dystopian vision of his novel Plastipocalypse. He dreams up the ideas for his stories while riding his bicycle or backpacking in the wilderness with his wife, Carol. Writing is only one of Doug's passions – he also plays a mean guitar for the rock band 'The Dirt Surfers' and is the best cross-country skier in Shiawassee Country, Michigan.

The Snow Tunnel

Cecil climbed up on a small three-legged stool to look at his mother. She was just lying there in the fancy case with an expression of boredom upon her overly-powdered face. He could tell other people were watching him by the little icy pricks he felt on the back of his neck. He didn't care. Mother was going away forever and this would be his last chance to see her. The night before, Cecil lay awake in bed all night wondering if he would be able to remember her. He had taken one of her fine hankies that smelled like lilac from her top drawer and it was now safely folded inside his pocket. Looking down upon her now, he stared at her face and burned her image into his brain until his head hurt. No one told him to move away. Everyone seemed sorry that Dillen Bowman and his six-year-old son had lost their wife and mother to pneumonia.

****

It was a very cold winter all over the northern half of the United States, and Michigan had been hit with storm after storm. Autumn was a glorious but brief flash of sun and falling leaves and there was six inches of snow on the ground by Halloween. The Thanksgiving holiday found the Bowmans in fine shape. Mother was the best cook in town. Her turkey and yams filled Cecil's stomach and put a smile on his face. Wonderful aromas drifted through the small-framed home. Cecil's Great Aunt Beatrice, their only relative living nearby, spent the day with them. After dinner they all played Parcheesi in front of the fireplace, with Cecil winning two games to his great enjoyment. Mother read Cecil a chapter from *Treasure Island* and put Cecil to bed as a very happy boy.

Dillen had steady work hauling lumber from Ortonville to Fenton, and even the deep snow couldn't keep his team of horses and sleigh from completing the hilly thirty-mile round trip every day, six days per week. But just a week before Christmas, Sophie Bowman acquired a terrible cough, which Dr. McGregor could do nothing about. He recommended bed rest, so Cecil and his father suffered with their own cooking. Dillen managed to get Cecil out of the house each morning for the long walk to school.

Cecil arrived home from school on December 22, 1906, to find his mother asleep. Their neighbor, Mrs. Tweety, checked up on Sophie during the day. There was a stew in the ice-box that Mrs. Tweety had left for them, so Cecil put it on the stove. Dad would be home soon and he was sure to be hungry after a cold, hard day out on the road.

Cecil went outside to work on the tunnel he had started the previous day. A massive snow drift had formed against the side of the house, perfect for a secret hideout. He imagined he was digging deep into the earth, and he would dig clean through to China. It was almost large enough to conceal his entire body. The isolation was calming. The whistling wind was quieted by the two-foot snow wall, making it a comfortable, safe place. Cecil had learned about Eskimos in his first grade class and was impressed with their way of life. Just dig a hole anywhere you want and you've got a nice and cozy place to live. After a half hour of digging Cecil had a fine tunnel. When it became too dark to see he went back into the house.

Cecil heard his father stomping the snow off his boots outside. The door opened, letting in a blast of icy air.

"Howdy, Son. How's your mother? She feeling any better?"

"She's been sleeping since I got home. I was quiet and let her rest."

"Good boy." Dillen went into the bedroom to check on his wife, and came back out into the kitchen immediately.

"Cecil, quick! Run and get the doctor."

"What's wrong, Dad?"

"Hurry! Don't ask questions!"

Cecil grabbed his coat and ran outside. He had on the homemade moccasins that his dad made for him, and he could feel the snow sliding up his pant legs. Twice Cecil tripped and fell in the deep drifts. Dr. McGregor lived about a mile away on the top of Detton Hill, and even though the temperature hadn't been much above ten degrees, Cecil dripped with sweat from the effort as he pounded on the door of the biggest house in Fenton.

"Doctor McGregor! Doctor McGregor!"

Inside the house, Dr. James McGregor was just finishing a dinner of roast venison and potatoes. He was used to interruptions at meal time and quickly answered the door. He looked down and saw a child covered with snow.

"Hello, Cecil. What's wrong?"

"I dunno. My dad says to come quick. It's Mother."

"Come in out of the cold for a moment while I get my things."

Cecil fidgeted, jumping from foot to foot, while waiting for the doctor to put on his coat and boots. "Hurry doctor. When Dad says to hurry, he means it!"

James chuckled to himself. "I know, I know. I'm sure your mother will be all right."

It would take longer to saddle up the horse than it would to walk, so the doctor and Cecil hurried to the Bowman house on foot. Cecil tried to follow the doctor, stepping in his footprints, but the doctor's stride was so long that Cecil had to jump from footprint to the next footprint. Soon he was tired of trying and just ran along beside the doctor.

"Doctor!" Dillen Bowman yelled as the doctor and Cecil entered the house. "She's not breathing!"

Dr. McGregor stomped the snow off his boots and threw his coat on a kitchen chair. He reached into his medical bag for his stethoscope and said to Dillen, "Leave the room for a moment while I examine her."

James feared the worst. What a shame for this young family to lose their wife and mother now, only days before Christmas. But death was an uncaring fellow who took whomever he wanted, whenever he pleased.

James left the bedroom, closing the door behind him. Dillen and Cecil stared at the doctor, unblinking. He hated this part of his profession. He personally knew each of his patients, he ate meals with them and most attended his church. Sophie Bowman had been the chairman of the doctor search committee who had brought him to Fenton, and she had been the first to welcome him as he stepped off the train two years ago. No finer woman had graced this community.

"I'm sorry. She's gone. There's nothing I could do."

Cecil looked up at his father. Not understanding, he said, "Dad? Where did she go?"

The big man was crushed. He collapsed into a kitchen chair and buried his face in his tired hands.

Now Cecil understood. The doctor bent down to try to explain things to the boy, but Cecil ran outside. He crawled into his Eskimo tunnel and cried.

****

Sophie Bowman would have been buried on Christmas Eve, but the ground was frozen. Cecil hid behind his father's leg as the sinister looking Mr. Crabnail, the village mortician, explained that he had a holding room for corpses.

"I'll bury a bunch of them as soon as the ground thaws," he said, lacking any resemblance of sympathy for the grieving. "I'll let you know when I put her in the ground. You'll want to have her marker ready by then."

Christmas Day was a fog of misery for Cecil and his father. Great Aunt Beatrice, too old to travel in such cold weather, was spending

Christmas Day with her next-door neighbors. Mrs. Tweety didn't want Cecil and Dillen to spend the day alone and invited them both over to her little house to share Christmas dinner with her and her husband, Elmer.

Just before departing, Dillen, with tears in his eyes, knelt by Cecil and said, "Son, I just don't feel up to being around other folks quite yet. You go on by yourself."

Cecil didn't quite know how to react. His father was crying! He quickly turned and left the house, leaving his father alone in his grief.

At the Tweety house, Cecil and Mr. and Mrs. Tweety enjoyed a fine meal of ham, potatoes, and pecan pie. At the conclusion of the meal, Mrs. Tweety, who had always been a kind and loving neighbor, reached into the pocket of her apron and withdrew a small wrapped gift and handed it to Cecil.

"Merry Christmas," Cecil. "Mr. Tweety and I got you a small gift."

Cecil anxiously unwrapped the package.

"It's a jack knife! Wow!" He opened up the three-inch steel blade and immediately sliced his finger. "Oh! It's sharp!"

"Come here, let me look at that." Mrs. Tweety wrapped a towel around the finger to slow the bleeding. "You'll have to be careful, Cecil. It's a tool, not a toy. Maybe you're too young for a knife."

It was the best gift Cecil had ever received, and he would die if Mrs. Tweety took it back. "I'll be really careful." The bleeding stopped, Cecil opened up the blade again, this time more carefully. "Thank you, Mrs. Tweety. Thank you, Mr. Tweety."

Elmer Tweety was a quiet man, but he had one thing to say. "You and that knife both learned a lesson. It's tasted your blood and now it knows who its owner is. You've felt its sting and now you will treat it with care and respect."

Cecil examined the knife, with its bone handle and shiny new blade.

"You hear that knife? You know who the boss is now," he said. "Do not bite me again."

Later that same evening, Cecil sat in front of the fireplace whittling away at a small piece of oak. When he was satisfied with the results, he gave the carving to his father.

"I didn't get you anything for Christmas, Dad, but I made you this. It will help you remember Mother."

The oak was in the shape of a heart. Carved carefully into the wood were the names "Dillen and Sophia."

Dillen could not bear to raise his tear-filled eyes to look up at the boy. "Merry Christmas, Dad. I did it in kind of a hurry, so it's not too good."

Cecil watched his father stare at the small carving. Tears streamed down Dillen's face.

"Oh Cecil, "Dillen cried. "I will never forget your mother, as long as I live!" He wrapped his arms around the small boy in a loving hug. "Thank you for this precious gift! This hasn't been much of a Christmas, but I will do everything I can to make sure that the next one is better."

Bedtime was approaching, and as Cecil made his way to the outdoor privy, he shrugged off the cold air and took a look at his snow tunnel. In the darkness he could no longer see the entrance. Drifting snow had completely erased any evidence of his work.

Maureen Bishop Gilna has been a member of the Shiawassee Area Writers since 2017.

She has been active in her church and community having resided in Owosso and Corunna all her life. She graduated from Owosso High in 1956.

Maureen pursued and received a Bachelor of Science Degree when she was 54-years-old. She has received many community awards of achievement throughout the years. She continues to serve her church and has been active in the Memorial Healthcare Hospice Program since 1981.

Through the years, Maureen has written poems and articles for various farm related newsletters and newspapers.

Her book, *Be Not Afraid,* was published in 2013. In that book, she shares the spiritual and miraculous moments of her near death experience.

Maureen lives with her husband, Richard, on the family farm in Corunna. They are the parents of four children and six grandchildren.

Maureen Bishop Gilna

Santa's Helpers

For my children- 1968

Up at the North Pole, a few years ago
Up on the ice and white fluffy snow
Santa sat in his workshop, a frown on his face
What could be his trouble in this cozy place

In walked his helper, Alfonso the Elf
He saw this sad Santa and said to himself
I must find out why Santa is so sad
I must find out now and I must make him glad

Santa, whatever can the matter be
Oh, little elf I cannot possibly see
How I can hear the wishes of children this year
What with all of the work I have to do here

Little Alfonso sat down and he thought
Oh, how hard for some answer he sought
Finally, an idea as bright as the sun
Came to his mind like a deer on the run

Remember your helpers up at Candycane Land
The ones who made toys before the season began
They have no work at all to do now
And will be delighted to help you somehow

On Santa's face appeared a big smile
He went to his desk and looked through his file
Yes, yes! he shouted, their names are all here
I will call them right now for Christmas is near

I must have helpers to sit in the stores
I need helpers to bring toys to the poor
Helpers are needed to ride in parades
That have various floats of beautiful shades
I must have helpers attend Christmas parties
Giving sweet candies and laughing so hearty

My helpers will dress the same as Santa would
With a heart full of love as we all know they should
All children must know that the secret they tell
To each Santa's helper will go pell mell

Straight to the North Pole by way of the phone
Right to my workshop where I'll be alone
I will put the secrets all here in my file
Then ring directly on my little elf dial
And ask for an elf whose job it is to see
That children are being as good as can be

Now I can return directly to my busy workshop
Making toys that will sing and toys that will hop
Thank you Alfonso, you have saved the day
I now know that Christmas will be ever so gay

So now boys and girls, you know when you see
A helper dressed the same as Santa would be
Whether he is big or tall or rather thin
Or short and squatty with a chubby chin
The secret you whisper into his ear
Will be the one that Santa receives this year
And if you are good, like I know you will be
You will find lots of surprises under your Christmas tree

Tracey Bannister works as a Mass Communication Specialist in the U.S. Navy.

She has published works online and in newsprint covering events for the Navy including exercises in the Baltic Sea, Japan and Pearl Harbor. She graduated with a Bachelor's degree in Journalism and Mass Communication at Ashford University and received a Bachelor's degree in Business Administration from Central Michigan University.

Bannister joined the Shiawassee Area Writers Group to help with her aspirations of working as an editor and eventually to write about her passions including true crime stories, military experiences, and her love of the outdoors.

She is a native of Midland, Mich. and currently resides in Owosso, Mich. You can read more works from this author at http://dreamcatcher.pressfolios.com/

A Snowy Gift

"You are never too old to set another goal, or to dream a new dream."
— C.S. Lewis

My favorite winter novel is The Lion, the Witch and the Wardrobe. It's not often thought of in the genre of winter themed novels, but it certainly holds a place in my heart. The main character, Lucy, discovers a wardrobe while playing hide and seek and chooses this as her hiding place. She steps into the wardrobe and starts walking backwards, drifting through the clothes and coats. As she continues, the clothes turn into pine branches covered with snow in a landscape unfamiliar to her.

Lucy has all the wonderment and excitement an innocent child would have entering a brand new world. This snowy world called Narnia is filled with magic, mythical beasts, and talking animals, but it's also filled with danger. The ice queen has put a spell on Narnia and has frozen the landscape, which results in the Hundred Year Winter. With the help of her siblings and under the guidance of Aslan, the Great Lion and guardian of Narnia, Lucy helps to cast aside the witch's spell and relieve Narnia of its perpetual winter.

My memories transported me back to the book as I stood in line outside the drill hall waiting for what seemed like forever. It was the day before my boot camp graduation. My division, along with several other divisions, waited to begin the rehearsal for graduation. The real ceremony was scheduled the next day and many of our family members and friends traveled long distances to attend.

It took a lot of hard work to get this far. Out of the 44 female recruits from my division that started this journey, only 24 remained. Injuries and failed qualifications took almost half of the recruits. Eight weeks of sunup to sundown training had taken its toll. We were physically and mentally exhausted. What should have been viewed as great personal triumphs were trivialized by our instructors, a tactic used to make recruits think they can always do better. All we could think of was the day we wouldn't have to be here anymore.

Chicago in October usually experiences autumn weather with leaves falling and mild temperatures with cold, crisp nights. However, on this unusual fall day, the temperature had dropped into the freezing range and snowflakes came down violently with the cold wind, stinging our faces. It felt like we were under the Witch of Narnia's spell. Our instructors were kind enough to make us dress as warm as the uniform policy allowed. We were completely covered in winter coats, scarves, hats, and mittens. I still froze though. The dress shoes offered only a thin layer to protect my feet from the elements. We were all miserable, or so I thought. All I could think was, *Oh great. Just what we need, a snowstorm in October.* After all we had been through, we were awarded with horrible weather.

That's when my roommate, born and raised in Miami, stood next to me and exclaimed, "Oh my goodness, it's snowing! It's so beautiful! I've never seen snow before!" I looked at her and saw the same childlike expression of wonder on her face as Lucy did in Narnia.

I grew up in Michigan where the winters can be brutal. My friends who have moved away often refer to it as the "frozen tundra," so it never occurred to me there might be people that had never seen snow. Up until that point, I had only focused on how cold it was and the hardships we had endured during our stay in boot camp, but the moment my roommate spoke up, my misery all but disappeared. I remembered what it was like to be a kid playing in the snow, holding your tongue out to catch the snowflakes and making snow forts and snow angels. The moment seemed surreal. It sent me back to those scenes in my favorite book and at that moment, I remembered why I was standing there. Like Lucy, I longed to see new places and find adventure and I had signed up to do just that by joining the Navy. The graduation ceremony marked the fulfillment of that dream. My adventure was just beginning.

Jodi Gerona is an aspiring author with a desire to share God through her writing. She works full time as a Data Quality Analyst and is the faithful wife of a fisherman and devoted mother of two young boys. She loves being with her family, enjoying the great outdoors and all 'Pure Michigan' has to offer.

Jodi Gerona

Unforgettable Winter

My journey began in the Lutheran Church where catechism classes and religious doctrine laid the foundation for my faith. Although raised and confirmed as a member, I never felt like I belonged. In 2004, shortly after getting married, my husband and I attended an Assembly of God church. We were welcomed into the church family and made it our worshiping home for seven years. Through attending church services, reading my Bible and spending time in prayer, I discovered faith is more about having a relationship with Jesus than religion.

In early 2011, following pastoral and other changes, we started searching for a new place to worship. In the year between making that decision and my dad getting sick, we visited several churches, but none felt like home. After several months, we decided to settle on one, but God had other plans.

In the winter of 2012, I experienced God on a personal level. He met our most pressing need and, in the process, led us to a new church. It was a winter I'll never forget.

February 18, 2012, we had a Valentine's Day dinner with friends. My mom and I shopped the night before for groceries. On our way to the store, I noticed a Pentecostal Church of God van. It sparked my interest because we were still exploring our church options.

After dinner the next evening, I received a phone call. It was unusual for my phone to ring that late and even more so that it was my mom who had just left with the other dinner guests. She was worried about my dad and thought he needed medical attention. He had been sick for a few weeks, losing weight and growing weaker by the day.

Prior to that, on a night Mom worked late, I called Dad to see if he needed anything. He said, "A new body." I told him I was praying for him and he said, "Thank you." I prayed for Dad every morning on my way to work. I prayed for his salvation, deliverance, and healing. I hoped somehow his illness would lead to a new beginning for him and our family.

That night, after dinner, Mom asked me to come over and convince Dad to go to the hospital. It was late, I was tired and didn't want to go anywhere except bed. She sensed my reluctance to brave the bitter cold and called his doctor for guidance. After talking with the doctor and several phone calls, back and forth, we decided to wait until morning.

My conscience nagged me, and I couldn't sleep. I got up, got dressed and headed to my parents' house. I stopped at the gas station on my way and pulled into a parking spot next to the church van I had seen the previous night.

When I got to the house, Dad was reclined in his chair, under a blanket, eating oatmeal. I had no idea why Mom was so concerned until he tried to talk. He didn't have enough breath or strength to finish his sentences. He was reluctant but we convinced him to head to the hospital.

In the process of checking vitals and poking and prodding, one of the nurses asked him what was going on. He said, "Too many years of body abuse." My heart broke at the sound of regret in his voice.

I spent President's Day at the hospital with Dad. I wanted to talk with him about Jesus. I wanted to know about his salvation and how he was feeling but I couldn't find the words. I didn't want to upset, hurt, or anger him. He had a hard time speaking anyway so we sat quietly and watched *Good Morning America*.

A headline appeared on the screen about the Queen's jubilee. It caught my attention because jubilee is not a word you see often but it was one of the words written on the side of the church van I had seen. Later that afternoon, we discovered Dad had cancer.

Wednesday, after work, I picked up my youngest son from the babysitter. I drove past a catering hall and had to do a double take when I read their sign. It was lit up at the side of the road and welcomed the

Pentecostal Church of God. It was the very same church I was reminded of by a news headline and whose van I had seen two nights in a row.

When I arrived at the hospital, Mom told me a friend of a friend offered to have her pastor visit Dad. When I shared with her about seeing the church name again on the sign, she responded, "You're never going to believe what church the pastor is coming from." Yes, it was, once again, the very same Pentecostal Church of God church that kept popping up wherever I went.

Dad's doctors wanted to determine the origin of his cancer. A lung scope was scheduled Thursday morning to help him breathe easier in preparation for more tests. They took him back for the procedure and decided he was too weak to have it done. There was nothing more they could do for him. Dad told the doctor he did not want to be resuscitated. I felt paralyzed and helpless as the nurse attached the purple DNR bracelet to his wrist. Dad was dying and there wasn't anything anyone could do.

Since we didn't have a pastor of our own, we requested one from the hospital. Two pastors came to talk and pray with us. One stood in the center of the room and the other just inside the door. They were more concerned about us than Dad. Neither one acknowledged him or asked about his salvation.

Later that night, the pastor from the Pentecostal Church of God stopped by the hospital. He introduced himself and walked right up to Dad's bedside. He asked if anyone knew for certain whether Dad would go to Heaven if he died that night. Sadly, we didn't know. He acknowledged Dad, talked to him, laid hands on him and prayed the salvation prayer with him. God sent the right person at the right time to meet our most pressing need that winter night.

Although, Dad could not interact with us, I knew he could still hear. I told him he would get that new body he wanted, a glorified body in Heaven, according to Philippians 3:32.

We didn't know how much time we had left with Dad. My mom,

brother, sisters and I stayed awake at the hospital all night. We shared memories, listened to music and read from the Bible. Mom was reminded of John 14:2 where it says, "My Father's house has many rooms; if that were not so, would I have told you that I am going there to prepare a place for you?" Looking back, it seems Jesus was preparing a place for Dad at that moment.

Exhausted from being up all night, I laid down in the other bed in Dad's room. That's where I was when he took his final breath, Friday, February 24, 2012. My heart was broken. Psalm 34:18, says the Lord is close to the broken hearted. God drew near in my time of need and comforted me.

My first comfort came in a dream where I was laying across a bed, face down and crying. I heard a voice say, "Don't cry, I'm okay." I lifted my eyes to see Dad standing there in his flannel pajamas and blue robe. He was young, healthy, and strong. Reminded me of pictures I had seen of him in his youth. It's an image that will stay with me forever.

For a while, after Dad died, I cried on my way to work. One brisk winter morning, I was overcome with grief for not sharing my faith and asking if he knew Jesus as his Savior. I could have been the one person standing between him and Heaven or Hell. I regretted not spending more time with him. Oh, how I wished for more time. All these thoughts, plagued with guilt and regret, consumed my mind until I glanced up and saw a glimmer of hope. Piercing through the gray, winter sky, appeared a small rainbow. Like in Genesis 9:13, a sign of God's promise, just for me. At that moment, a comforting peace came over me and I knew Dad had gone home to be with the Lord in Heaven.

At some point, I started to question why God didn't heal Dad and give him a new beginning and more time. When my grief turned to anger, God opened my eyes to see that Dad had been saved, healed, and delivered. God answered my prayers, just not how I wanted. Isaiah 55:8, tells us God's ways are better than our ways. Even when things don't go the way we want, or how we plan, God is working it out for our good, like it says in Romans 8:28. We don't have to understand it all, we just need to have faith and believe.

Although God comforted me, I struggled with Romans 10:9-10, which says, "If you declare with your mouth, "Jesus is Lord," and believe in your heart that God raised him from the dead, you will be saved." Dad physically could not speak during the salvation prayer. I shared my concern with friends who reassured me that although he couldn't say the prayer with his physical body, he was alive, and his spirit was able to receive the gift of salvation. I appreciated their explanation but still worried until God reminded me that Dad had acknowledged Jesus as Lord when he thanked me for praying for him.

Matthew 11:28, says "Come to me, all you who are weary and burdened, and I will give you rest." Dad is resting in the arms of our Savior. He is no longer weary and burdened. He received his new beginning in Heaven and we received a new beginning in the Pentecostal Church of God. At this church, I learned about the power of the Holy Spirit, received the baptism of the Holy Spirit and experienced the movement of the Holy Spirit.

God carried me through that winter by giving me exactly what I needed, when I needed it. He is good and faithful, in every season, to meet our needs and guide our journey. Each church served as a stepping stone in my faith walk, drawing me closer to God and into a deeper relationship with Jesus. It is because of Jesus, I have hope. Hope of eternal life found in Titus 1:2.

Shawn Gallagher is a retired teacher with a Master's Degree in Special Education from Michigan State University. She currently works as a homeschool teacher and educational therapist to students on the autism spectrum. She enjoys sharing her love of writing and storytelling with the young people she teaches. In addition to her personal writing, she collaborates with her pupils on short stories, essays, greeting cards, limericks and lyrics to corny ukulele songs.

Room at the Inn

We thought the old Cutlass would get us safely home for Christmas. In December of 1976, my older sister Colleen and I finished our college classes and left Kalamazoo, Michigan for the two-hour drive east. It was late evening. We pooled the scant cash we had and bought just enough gas to make the trip to the Detroit suburbs. Neither of us owned a credit card, and mobile phones were a device of the future. Colleen and I knew the car had sputtered on occasion, but it always started without fail, and we had no concerns as we drove along and discussed our holiday plans. Like many of our friends from school, we gave little thought to weather forecasts and were dressed for comfort in the car, which meant light jackets and sneakers.

We were an hour into our drive as evening turned to night, and an earlier sprinkling of flurries became a steady and heavy snow. Out of the blue, the car began to clank and grind.

"What was that?"

"I'm not sure, but it's done that before. No worries." My sister spoke with confidence. It seems unbelievable now that we drove without care in deteriorating conditions without even a basic knowledge of car maintenance, unaware of how to change a tire, locate a dipstick or, more crucially, analyze the seriousness of a clanking engine. Emergency money was not a thought. We both worked part-time and were barely scraping by. Road service club dues were unaffordable.

We made it about sixty miles. In pitch black darkness and now blinding snow, the car halted somewhere in rural Washtenaw County. Puzzled, we decided to lock the doors, turn on the hazard lights—at least we knew where those were—and wait for help to arrive.

"I think we're supposed to stay in the car until the police come," Colleen announced in a calm tone. That sounded like a reasonable plan.

The heater had quit, so it didn't take long for the cold to become uncomfortable. As we waited, past newspaper headlines began to creep into my thoughts. People froze to death in stranded cars, buried alive in piles of snow. Surprisingly few motorists passed by, and none of them noticed us. It was the type of weather where most folks were singularly focused on getting to their destinations. Plus, you never knew who was in a stalled car. There had been a string of co-ed killings in Ann Arbor in the late 1960's, and this was still a frightening memory for many. People were cautious about stopping for strangers.

After about twenty minutes, it was clear that we would have to rescue ourselves. Colleen voted to stay with the car. We could see no houses, only trees and fields. Born and raised in big cities, we were uneasy with open, unpopulated areas. We waited a bit longer. The cold became unbearable. I decided to voice my fear. "People freeze to death in cars. I think we should get out. No one is even looking our way." Had this also crossed Colleen's mind? I watched as she scanned the area with a wide-eyed nervous expression. Then she pointed out a faint, distant light on the other side of I-94.

"That might be a house . . . with a phone," I suggested. That was all it took. We grabbed our purses and stepped out to face the weather and the interstate. We had four lanes of slippery roads to cross and minimal chance of being seen in the dark, white-out conditions. We crossed the eastbound lanes, shuffling and sliding, determined not to fall. When we reached the median, we climbed down, then up, the snow-covered embankment. Terrified, we traversed the westbound lanes and reached a several-acre field. A barbed-wire fence surrounded it—a very unwelcome sight. Climbing over was not an appealing option, but the good news was there was indeed a house, and a light was on inside. We made it over the fence and trudged onward.

The field was now blanketed by several inches of snow. Gloveless hands in pockets, feet in flimsy shoes and fearful of encounters with wild critters, we sank into knee-deep drifts and painstakingly made our way to the porch. Numb and out of breath, we reached the door. Colleen glanced at her watch. It was 9 p.m.

"What if these people are shady?" I whispered as Colleen pressed the doorbell. We surveyed the area. The nearest home was at least a half-mile away. With no choice but to proceed, we waited for a response. No answer. We rang again. Please be home. We were shivering, exhausted and had no back-up plan. On the third ring, a curtain moved aside and the door opened a crack. What if they won't let us in? Two frightened-looking senior citizens peered through the opening and asked what we wanted.

"Our car broke down on the highway. Could we please use your phone?" They hesitated. Neither my sister nor I had considered that they might be afraid of us, but huddled together in the narrow opening, the man's arm protectively around the woman's shoulders, that appeared to be the case. Uh-oh. We'd better sound convincing.

"Would you please call the police or a tow truck?" Colleen extended her driver's license. The seconds ticked by as they looked us over. We must have seemed wet and miserable enough that they decided to take a chance. As the old couple slowly opened the door, I calculated that my job was to stay near the entry and appear non-threatening and polite. They led Colleen to the kitchen and the phone. She would call the towing company and then our parents. Red-faced with embarrassment, we realized these long-distance calls would incur a charge for our hosts, and we had no money to offer. Dad would have to take care of it when he arrived. The old gentleman dialed the towing company first and handed the phone to Colleen. The news wasn't good. All of the trucks were out on runs, and the dispatcher had no idea when one would become available.

"This is a pretty bad storm, you know—lots of crashes and cars in ditches tonight. Probably won't get to yours until morning." He gave no false hope. This was unexpected, but at least it was the weekend. Dad would have time to bring us back for the car tomorrow. My sister thanked the homeowners and asked to call our parents. She offered to call collect, but they refused. I bet they want to hurry us along so they can go to bed. I walked into the kitchen in order to hear. As I listened to Colleen explain the situation to Mom, I estimated how long it would take Dad to make the trip. She glanced at me with a look that announced we were in trouble. Her chin quivered and her voice shook as she tried to maintain her composure.

"When is he coming?" I mouthed. She shook her head.

"Not coming," she whispered, looking defeated. What did she mean? I'll take care of this. I reached for the phone.

"Mom, what's going on?" I snapped with impatience.

"Your dad is not here. He's hours away on work business. I'm alone with your five brothers and sisters. I can't come for you. Why did you start out so late?" There was a hint of blame.

"But what are we supposed to do? The car is dead and we have no money." I was no longer maintaining appearances in front of the couple. We needed to get out of there.

"You'll figure it out. Ask if you can stay there." She could not be serious. We can't impose on these people this way. I was mortified. It was one thing to interrupt their evening, scare them to death and run up phone charges. It was another to ask to stay in their home. Reality quickly set in. We didn't have money for a hotel. There was no hotel; we were nowhere near a town. We had no transportation. It was humiliating to accept, but our predicament was clear. The only question was who would make the awful request. With my silence, I chose Colleen. She was the more convincing of the two of us, I rationalized. In truth, I simply could not say the words. What if they said no? They had every right to refuse. They were already anxious and had been more than generous. Where would we go? Back across the field to the highway to try our luck starting the car? I could feel tears pooling in my eyes. I was cold, tired, angry with my parents for letting us down and ashamed to have to rely on the pity of others.

The couple stared at each other. I stood motionless then gave a slight nod to my sister. Go on, I implied. She was trembling. She's the oldest, I told myself. She cleared her throat and choked out the words.

"Do you think we could stay here tonight?" There it was--the surrender of pride, the admission of defeat. Silence followed.

"Would you excuse us for a moment?" the wife asked. We sat in the dim light of the spotless kitchen while our fate was decided.

"Are you sure you don't have any money?" Colleen was desperate.

"No, I don't. We spent it all on gas, remember?"

At last the couple returned, and with the hoped for words. "You are welcome to stay here tonight." Oh thank you, God.

"We cannot tell you how much we appreciate this." I nearly sobbed. Thanks seemed inadequate. They led us to a charming room decorated with country touches and wished us a good night. Suddenly too wired to sleep, I examined our lodgings. No television, no radio, just a comfortable double bed in a warm house, safe from the storm. It was all we really needed. It took a while to quiet my racing thoughts about what the next day would bring. Would the snow stop? Would we be able to get a tow truck? How would we get back to school if the car couldn't be repaired? Fatigue finally won, and before I knew it, the sun shone through the window, and the delicious aroma of pancakes and sausage floated into the room.

We ate the tasty breakfast. When had our last meal been? Our hosts couldn't have been nicer. They were probably relieved we weren't thieves trying to pilfer their valuables. After our meal, we made another call home. This time Dad answered and the husband gave him directions. The next call was for a tow truck. The same man who took the call the night before agreed to meet us at the car. A couple of hours later, Dad arrived.

"Thank you for taking care of my girls. I'd like to pay you for your trouble."

They politely declined. "We were happy to do it. We have children, too."

The tow truck driver said he'd passed our car several times during the night. "I looked for it when I heard your story. Must have a good battery; the hazard lights stayed on all night."

The car was repaired in time for us to return to school. A few months later, it would roll across the parking lot of Colleen's apartment complex during the night and knock another vehicle down a hill. Some cars are just bad news.

In later years, Colleen and I reminisced about the Christmas incident and about how casually it seemed Mom had told us, "You'll figure it out." She hadn't panicked, hadn't offered a list of solutions and didn't call around to find help for us. What mother reacts that way, we wondered. Turns out it was a mother with seven children who married at 19 and had her first child at 20. She had lost her own mother as an infant and was raised by her grandmother, who was in her seventies when Mom had her first baby, Colleen. Mom was expected to "figure things out" in navigating marriage and motherhood at the same age my sister and I were able to enjoy the relative freedom of college. She had the same confidence in the abilities of her two oldest to survive that her grandmother had in her.

We discovered later that Mom had sent a letter of gratitude to our "innkeepers." Maybe the two farmers could relate to raising large families and facing adversities, for they exchanged Christmas cards with Mom and Dad for many years.

Cheers

May the trunk of your tree
Always fit in the stand
And every bulb stay lit
On your fifty-foot strand

Hope Christmas songs don't
Begin in October
Pray the cat doesn't knock
The nativity over

May you write the most witty
Of family letters
And get oohs and ahs
On your holiday sweaters

Here's hoping you don't
Re-gift the fondue
To the one who originally
Gave it to you

Beware of the sly old
Mistletoe creep
Who pounces with bad breath
And cologne that smells cheap

Don't drink any eggnog
That's flavored with rum
A stumble means pine needles
Stuck in your bum

Hope someone gifts you
A lottery winner
So you can treat friends
To a seven-course dinner

Have a party that's free
Of a large family brawl
Peace, joy and cheers
Merry Christmas to all

Cyndy Habermehl is a graduate of Baker College, Owosso, with an Associate of Applied Science Degree. After thirty years working in the medical field, Cyndy is now enjoying her retirement years by writing memoirs, poetry and children's books. She lives with her husband, Lee, and they both live near the farm she grew up on, also where these stories originated.

A Christmas Doll

My memories of Christmas past are of cold days on the farm where I grew up. Chores were an everyday occurrence, and I enjoyed being outdoors and carrying out my assigned jobs. My dad was a farmer from his birth. My mother learned to be a farm wife after marrying my dad at age seventeen and moving to the family farm. Being the oldest child of three, it was expected that I would do my share of the work to keep home and farm running. This included household as well as chores in the barns, taking care of the animals and many other odd jobs a child of my age could do, like putting out hay for the cows and straw in the cow stalls.

It was not all hard work, though. As the days of December were shorter and colder, we would find ourselves in the house more. My grandmother lived just down the road on the next farm, and she was the organist at the Durand Methodist Church. She would often come up on the hill where we lived and practice songs on the organ for Sunday worship service. I liked to hear her play, as she would add grace notes and extra flourishes to the songs. She was very talented. It would make me wonder how she could play without looking at her hands, all the while smiling and looking at me. Often she would play some children's songs I learned at church, like *Jesus Loves Me*, and in the season of Christmas, she would play any Christmas songs I requested, like *Frosty the Snowman*, *Jingle Bells* or *Away in a Manger*. I enjoyed the times when I would climb up with her on the organ bench and snuggle close. It made me feel special and loved to sit there and watch her fingers glide over the keys.

At Christmastime, my mom would decorate the house and I would help. I liked the singing angels she put on the aged wooden radio cabinet in the living room. The Christmas tree was decorated with old colored light bulbs and silver tinsel. We then added the ornaments collected over the years by my mom and Dad.

As Christmas Eve came, the excitement in our house grew as we anticipated what Santa would bring us. It was my dad's custom that each of us three kids get a dining room chair, pull it into the living room and line them up in a row, with a small space left between chairs. Then we would hang our stockings on the back of the chairs and use large diaper pins to hold them in place. Each of our stockings had our name embroidered on the upper cuff which my mother had stitched. This way Santa could find the proper chair for each of us. After we placed Christmas cookies on a plate, along with a tall glass of milk, we would head upstairs to our beds. Mom and Dad said prayers with us and tucked us in for the night.

It was hard falling asleep, not only with the excitement of Santa's arrival but the farmhouse was colder upstairs than downstairs. Even with flannel pajamas, footies, and warm blankets, a little shivering would go on before finally falling asleep.

On one Christmas morning I heard Mother call softly up the stairs, "Wake up kids, come down and see what Santa has left you, he has been here." With excitement, I sprang from my bed and quickly descended the stairs. Upon nearing the living room, the light was on, and at first look, it was a Christmas wonder and surprise. The Christmas tree lights were on and the chairs were covered with toys. The living room smelled like a fresh pine forest from the decorated real tree.

I looked closer at my chair and my eyes were quickly taken to a large box standing next to it on the floor. In the box, to my surprise and delight, I could see through the cellophane the most beautiful doll I had ever laid eyes on. She had blonde hair with a veil on her head and the most elegant bridal gown I had ever seen.

I paused a moment. I almost didn't want to touch her, or to open the box. I was thinking I might break her. I am not sure how long I stared, but I finally came forward and picked her up. She felt a little wobbly inside the box, so I set the package back down and proceeded to open the top of the box. Touching her veil and her face, I felt so happy. She was mine.

By then, my dad had noticed my hesitance to finish taking her out of the box. He reached over for the box and took out his pocket knife and eventually freed the doll from the packaging. He placed her into my arms. She was beautiful. She had the nicest smile on her face and I loved that she had blue eyes, like my own.

I know that I must have gotten other gifts that Christmas but the bride doll was my favorite. When I think of Christmas past, I remember this Christmas first of all and my beautiful bride doll.

Cyndy Habermehl

A Trip to The Sugarbush

I grew up on a farm in mid Michigan. I enjoyed the times I spent with my grandparents who lived next door. I would go along with them to work in the barn, feeding the sheep and cattle. They would also take me to the field when they were working there. The sights and sounds were amazing. Grandpa would tell me stories of his life on the farm, and I would ask him questions about our family and the generations who had lived on the farm before us. Time seemed to pass quickly as we worked and talked together.

I recall one winter when snow had freshly covered the ground. It must have been March. I think I was seven or eight years old. My grandparents and I took the John Deere tractor and the attached green wagon and went to their wooded property just down the road. My grandfather and grandmother called the woods "The Sugarbush."

As we neared the woods, my grandfather slowed the tractor down. We entered the wooded area carefully because there were several fallen limbs and rocks in the woods that had to be avoided. As we drove deeper into the woods, I could see the larger maples had galvanized metal buckets that were hanging from their trunks. Each bucket was hung by a spile which had been driven into the tree. A spile is like a metal straw that allows sap to flow from inside the tree and drip into the bucket. Drip, drip, drip. This would continue until the bucket was nearly full of sap. The sap was clear with an amber tint. It was sticky to the touch.

Grandfather parked the tractor and wagon over by a building they called "The Sugar Shack." It was not a fancy structure, just some weathered wood and an old board roof with a brick chimney. The smells that would come from there were amazing. There was the smoke from the fire burning inside and coming out of the chimney. Then there was the sweet smell of the sap cooking down into maple syrup.

That morning, my grandmother took a bucket from each tree and carried it to my father, who had arrived out in the woods before us. As she handed the bucket to him, he took the bucket inside the shack and Grandfather then began to cook down the sap. He handed the empty bucket back to Grandmother and she placed it back on the spile she had removed it from.

My grandmother had given me instruction that I was only to watch. I was not to take a bucket from the tree, that she would do that. This went on as she instructed for awhile, until she turned her back. I felt I could be helpful and do it myself. As I lifted the bucket, it got stuck on the spile groove and all that cold, cold sap began to run down the front of me, dousing me. I shouted, "Oh no!" Grandmother turned to see that I was clutching a nearly empty bucket and frozen, not knowing how to get myself out of this fix. She was not far away and ran over to take the bucket and save me, but I could tell she was not pleased. She was never one to scold or spank me, but I wish she would have said something to diffuse the stress of the situation.

As I was getting colder now that I was soaked, she took me home on the tractor and got me cleaned up and I put on some dry clothes.

A bit later we went back to the woods and finished making the maple syrup. Boy, was it ever delicious. It's times like this that I remember how good it was to grow up on a farm and how blessed I am to have such a wonderful family.

Elizabeth Wehman is the President of the Shiawassee Area Writers Group which she started in May of 2017.

Since 2014, she has three inspirational fiction works entitled *Under the Windowsill*, *Promise at Daybreak*, and *Just a Train Ride*. She is currently working on a sequel to *Just a Train Ride* set for publication in fall of 2018.

Elizabeth has been the editor of The Independent Newspaper and worked as a news reporter for two local newspapers for over ten years. She also has been published in many magazines, online publications, and has been a contributing writer for Union Gospel Press.

Wehman established her own publishing company in 2014. Summit Street Publishing will soon be helping other writers to fulfill their author dreams. Growing up in Lennon, she graduated from Durand High School and received a Bachelor's degree from Cedarville University. She currently lives in Owosso with her husband, David. You can find more about this author at www.elizabethwehman.com or on Facebook at Elizabeth Wehman/Author.

Elizabeth Wehman

The Winter of Life

'I know that nothing is better for them than to rejoice, and do good in their lives, and also that every man should eat and drink and enjoy the good of all his labor – it is the gift of God.'

Today's my birthday. Guests crowd the dining hall. Green and yellow paper streamers drape from the ceiling like a circus tent. I gaze into the flicker of fire coming from each candle as those gathered around me begin to sing the familiar tune. I've heard the melody for ninety plus years.

Everyone tried to warn me that old age would descend like winter, but living life stopped me from heeding the warning. Who listens to the elderly anyway? They prattle on about how it used to be, how it needs to be, what it should be. Life is life. Multiple seasons looped together by hours, days, months, and years.

Wasn't it just yesterday that I was at my childhood home longing for adulthood? Soon I would gather my meager belongings to head out into the world right after high school, anticipating the moment I could marry the love of my life, trusting her labor pains to bring a new life into the world. Most of life is an eagerness for the next big moment, adventure, and season. Now I desire country-fried steak for lunch and to watch out the window in hopes of a visitor, longing like anything to return to the golf course for one more putt on a green.

Yet I find myself, almost thirty years past retirement, gazing out a single-room window waiting for a cheerful bird to land on the sill. I realize the most comfortable place for me to sit is now a wheelchair. I'm in the winter of my life. Gone are the days of imagining what my future will hold. For now, there is nothing left to look forward to, only memories on which to reflect.

Birthdays flash before me as I study each candle. I remember the red bike I got when I turned seven and how anxious I was to learn to ride it without training wheels. I recall when I turned sixteen and asked my father to borrow the car after earning my license. I think of the surprise birthday on my fortieth, and the celebration of a trip to Hawaii on my sixtieth.

As I glance around the room, I'm grateful for all the family and friends who have been a part of my life. Each one now staring at me as though I'm supposed to entertain them by saying something profound. What could I say but what many tried to tell me at each stage of my life? Enjoy this time. Savor this stage. Kiss that lovely wife of yours, every single day.

I see the reflection of my life in their eyes. All younger than me. There are John and Arthur, friends from high school, but I think both of them were a grade behind me. All the way down to my great-great grandson now cradled in my great-granddaughter's arms. Many can recall how we met, and what happened in the season I shared with them, all in my ninety-two years on earth.

I see the co-worker who had to put up with my infatuation with donuts in the morning, to the neighbor who graciously brought me dinners after my latest hip surgery. Some, like my children, know me the best, yet so many are missing. Five years ago, I lost the love of my life. I knew she'd be front and center during this celebration, at my side, fingers intertwined. Oh how I wish I could be with her again, especially on my birthday.

The noise of singing comes to an end. Everyone watches in anticipation as I gather enough breath to blow out the candles on the cake. I manage to blow most of them out. My great-great grandson finishes the job with a bit of spit and vigor. I laugh. He reminds me of his father, yet as he looks up at me for approval, I even see myself. With a pat on his shoulder I whisper, "Good job." His return smile lights up my world better than any birthday candle.

I hadn't had this much attention since scoring the winning goal at the rivalry football game in the field south of town. Should I say something? How do you talk about an entire lifetime in a sentence or two? I replace the impossible task with a slow nod and a smile.

Inside, I feel no older. I still desire to grab a surfboard and head out into the ocean to catch a wave. Now, I'm happy when I can catch the attention of a nurse in the hall, not to give her a line of my best flirt, but so she can assist me to the bathroom. Blowing out candles leaves me breathless and tired. And I hurt. Everywhere.

My son approaches and asks, "Okay, Dad?" I nod. I'm really not, but the family had been so kind to throw such a celebration for me. But the honest truth is...I'd rather be in my room watching the next re-run of Bonanza.

They mean well and I'm grateful for the gestures of kindness, but having thirty minutes to tell them why I voted for the last President brings me greater joy than having to celebrate another birthday. Every year I'm uncertain if it will be my last. I may never have this many loved ones in a room until it's a memorial of my life instead of a celebration of another year. But that's how it is when you're old. Like me.

Well-wishers come now one by one to shake my hand. Some share a memory or two of our times together. Even though my desire is to be left alone mainly because I hear very little of what they have to say. My hearing aids pick up every noise in the room, causing a cacophony of blurred sounds. However, it is still nice to see everyone.

I wish for someone to ask me what I want for my big day. One thing is for sure, I'd be able to tell them. First, I want chocolate. I only have two or three peanut butter cups leftover from Christmas. Next, I'd rather have each family member choose days to visit me instead of gathering all at once. But last of all, I'd wish for a few moments with my sweetheart. Before I drift off to sleep each night I smile as I realize, with fondness, that I'm closer to being with her than I was the morning before.

I need to remind myself, a tad shy of a mere century, to take every day as a blessing from God. Encourage others to get up each morning and be happy to go to school, to work, to go on vacation. Treat each moment as something special, even the trying days, because that's what a day will hold. Joy. Frustrations. Thankfulness. Heartache. Happiness. For me, it's to gaze at yet another sunrise.

Appreciate each season more than the one before. For spring, summer, and fall fly by, and before you know it...winter will arrive. 'To everything there is a season, a time for every purpose under heaven.'

Take the time to play with your toddler. Stop long enough from fixing your car to enjoy day's sunset. Take a walk instead of driving to the store. Spend that savings on that convertible. Because it's true. Life is but a moment in time. An amazing gift. Cherish each day.

A Basement Christmas

Sounds of splintering wood followed by distinct glass-shattering crashes caused us to startle awake. Jolted out of bed by the noise, we couldn't imagine what was happening in our small December Michigan world, but whatever it was, we'd never heard anything like it before.

Gazing out a window, we discovered a world layered in glistening ice. As if we went to sleep during a winter storm and night had transported us to a frozen, magical, Disney-like world. As much as two or three inches encrusted every tree and bush, the ground appeared as frozen lakes. Our family of four had gone to bed with a forecast of sleet. The result was mystifyingly beautiful; another crash sent us rushing to the next window.

Across the street from our home were giant, grand oak trees, their glazed limbs drooping under the weight, many splitting as we watched...yet shimmering in the sunlight. The sight was breathtaking. The sun reflected a rainbow of light prisms from the jagged ice like diamonds under a jewelry store display case.

Despite the beauty of the glistening world, another large branch ripped from a tree and crashed to the icy earth, the silence of the still morning broken by the intense impact. As mystifying as it sounded, it was heartbreaking to witness. Coated electric and telephone wires resulted in no power to our water pump, no electricity to turn on a light, and an eerie quiet over the neighborhood.

I realized attending church wasn't an option. Today would have been a special service due to the upcoming holiday. Perhaps the warmth of the sun could melt the layers caused by the storm before the big day. I hoped to bake cookies for Christmas, a mere three days away. But from the look of it, baking anything would have to wait.

We lit a match to manually ignite the burners on the gas stove to boil water to give the kitchen a small source of heat.

We prepared a simple breakfast before my husband headed out to the barn to discover more storm damage. I watched him inch his way on the ice to the barn, in a skate-like walk. He reported back, "It's bad, but strangely beautiful."

Despite the sunshine, our home's temperature dropped degree by degree. My heavy winter robe would soon need to be layered with additional clothing. The dog crept out to "do his business" while the rest of the family stood at the patio door to watch him struggle and slip across the back deck in search of a place to get a foothold. Out of necessity, he did his best, returning in bewilderment with his tail wagging, happy to be back inside.

Our phones held bars from the night charges, and my son logged onto the power company's website for a possible prediction as to when our electricity might return. The report seemed inaccurate, as it reflected a six-day wait. Certainly that couldn't be true, but after another glance at the havoc the storm had left behind, we had a feeling that it might have caused more damage than we could see from our windows. Checking the weather predictions, we realized that Christmas week of 2013, in our part of the world, could possibly plunge us into subzero temperatures.

What could we do? We closed doors to unused rooms, gathered candles for the approaching night, even lit the stove for a little heat while we boiled water. Sadness crept in at the possibility of having to spend Christmas Day away from home. But where? Everyone else in the immediate area was in the same precarious situation.

We had company coming for Christmas Eve. How much food could you cook on a stove top? We couldn't flush toilets. With Christmas three days away, the refrigerator was packed with essentials to prepare the holiday meals. Our Christmas lights no longer twinkled on our tree. The storm left us in mental and physical turmoil.

A neighbor loaned us a small generator. My husband returned to the barn for gasoline left from summer lawn mowing. He added gas to the generator. Now we would at least preserve our food in the refrigerator and have a small heater for the dining room. We added more layers of clothing.

The short December daylight left us, the small generator provided the only noise. We'd retreat in the house just long enough to get warm, then have to head out to add more gas to the tank. If the ice wasn't enough, old man winter added snow and dropping temperatures into the single digits. The snow swirled around us as I held the siphon in place so my husband could add gas to the tank. Each trip was so cold that our few minutes inside weren't enough to get warm before having to head out again.

My husband and two children gathered with me in the living room with blankets and candles. Phones and devices lost charges, and we grew too cold to fill the generator any longer, the only thing left to do was head to bed early. At least the flannel and down comforters would give our icy fingers and noses some warm relief.

Although we slept better than expected, it was a difficult choice to remove the covers to face another day. The next day was colder than the previous one. We now wore winter coats indoors. As the second night of our frozen adventure descended we worried how much longer we could endure. It wasn't long before we realized it would be our last night at home. Despite all the extra blankets and heavy comforters, the cold took control.

One of the local hotels, which still had electricity, was full of stranded families from all over the community. Friends had visitors at their homes for Christmas, so their extra rooms were all taken.

That afternoon we discovered our church, a mere fifteen minutes away, hadn't lost power. The basement had a large kitchen, plumbing, and a community room. It might be fun to invite our family there instead of suffering in our frigid home.

Roads had cleared up a bit on Christmas Eve, so we loaded our Suburban with gifts and holiday food and headed to the warmth and convenience of the church. After the family celebration that afternoon, we would search for another place to stay. We didn't want to intrude on others for Christmas morning. We desired to celebrate Christmas as a family.

At the church, we unloaded the car, placed our Christmas Eve and day dinners in the refrigerator, and brought a decorated tree from the upstairs sanctuary down into our now warm, makeshift living quarters.

The family gathering went well and I asked my husband, "Do you think we could spend the night here?"

He replied, "In the church basement?"

"It's warm, the toilets flush, and everything is here that we need. An oven to cook the turkey. A large screen to watch a Christmas Eve movie. We can retrieve our family presents from home. What more could we ask for?"

He nodded, "I'll ask the Pastor."

He returned to announce, "It's ours for the holiday."

I'd done many things in the basement of our church from parties, children's church activities-I'd even cleaned it a few times-but I'd never before slept there. We inflated mattresses before heading home to gather more blankets and transport our remaining gifts to the comfortable, new living quarters. My son set up his computer so we could watch a holiday movie on a pull-down screen on the wall opposite our beds. Turning off all the lights, we admired our makeshift setting. It was Christmas Eve in a familiar place, but not our home. As adventurous and cozy as it was, I missed being home with our normal Christmas traditions.

The next day I prepared the turkey, made up a few salads and then realized that perhaps there were other church members displaced by the storm. When I mentioned this to my husband he added, "Let's ask them to join us."

We made some phone calls and found five other couples residing at a nearby hotel. We invited them to join us for Christmas dinner.

Our family enjoyed a morning to open gifts and celebrate before the others arrived. That afternoon we gathered four other couples, a single elderly woman, and our family for a Christmas Day dinner in the basement of the church.

We stayed two more nights in the comfort of the church basement. We knew we couldn't stay through the weekend, so we prayed our electricity would return. I needed to do laundry, and our groceries were all but gone. My husband headed home to check on our cold, frozen dwelling one more time. We didn't want our pipes to freeze. Before long he called to announce, "The electricity is back on."

Our prayers were answered right there in the church basement no far below where we worship each week. We were able to return to our house to see our decorations once again glowing on the remaining ice outside as well as a sweet reflection of lights from within our home. What a welcome sight.

Each Christmas, from that point on, we fondly reflect on our Christmas in the church basement. Was it our favorite? To be honest, no. We'd rather have been in our home, enjoying the day, but living at the church gave us perspective to be thankful in hard times and in all things. We had the opportunity to share our Christmas dinner with those who found themselves alone, too. And we also think of it in wonder. Christmas in the church basement; it makes for an adventurous, amazing story to tell.

The writers of the Shiawassee Area Writers would like to thank you for purchasing and reading our first anthology. Some of the proceeds from the book sales will be used toward scholarships for area students who are pursuing a career in journalism, literature, or creative writing.

Because everyone…has a story to share!

Made in the USA
Lexington, KY
08 October 2018